Money Island

TROY

The Larry Czerwonka Company, LLC
Hilo, Hawai'i

This is a work of fiction. Names, characters, businesses, places, events and incidents are either the products of the author's imagination or used in a fictitious manner. Any resemblance to actual persons, living or dead, or actual events is purely coincidental.

First Edition — September 2014

Published by: The Larry Czerwonka Company, LLC
http://thelarryczerwonkacompany.com

Printed in the United States of America
ISBN: 0692283129
ISBN-13: 978-0692283127

This book is dedicated to the dreamer in all of us.

To those who directed ours lives, those who influenced our lives.

To those that made us better.

To John and Koen for the kick-start.

This book is for those who think that limitations is just a word in the dictionary.

To my wife and my son.

Contents

Think Fast

"Yo, punk!" directed the hooded aggressor. He positioned himself between two cars to prevent the couple from reaching the street. The sound of the cars passing slowly by made it hard to fully understand what was happening. It was night and a Friday only made certain that some degree of chaos would be in the air.

"Look, white boy! I got a gun, let's make this easy."

The intended victim refused to make eye contact. Instead, he grabbed the hand of his female companion and pulled her to his face. Through his tight lips, he focused directly into her face. She wanted to speak, but her fear was too great and she looked to him for help. Instead, he mouthed to her a simple, yet forceful, "don't speak."

"Punk ass." The younger agitator again forced himself. "Talkin' to you, not her."

The intended victim still refused to make eye contact and continued looking away almost as if he didn't know they were there. He looked around the street hoping to see a policeman. Nothing. He looked back to the restaurant they had just left and caught the eye of the doorman only thirty feet away. He could not yell but instead he appeared to blow a kiss back to the Nigerian doorman. The doorman appeared confused and looked back at the couple.

A second agitator spoke up and challenged his friend. "Hey man, he ignoring you. Pop 'em."

Sensing he needed to act quickly, the victim again pulled his female companion to his side and turned to face the two threatening him. It was the first time he had dared to make eye contact.

"I got a gun, gimme your wallet. You, too," the agitator coolly spoke and then moved toward the female. "Gimme now."

"Man, we ain't scared to do this here," added the second agitator.

The man looked at the two and tried to make out their faces behind the hoodies and then offered his first words. "I can't hear you, I'm deaf." He motioned his hands in a made up sign language that only he knew.

His monotone voice surprised the assailants and momentarily disarmed them, they looked at each other in a what-to-do moment. The male pulled his female friend to his back in an attempt to protect her. The first agitator turned and said "You deaf?"

To which the older male victim nodded and repeated, "I'm deap." In his attempt to appear disabled, he mispronounced the word in hopes of gaining some sympathy. It did not work.

The assailant reached in his waistband, produced a small pistol and put it into the face of the victim. "Deaf? Then this is going to be easy."

Those were his last words as a powerful fist struck the assailant's face. As the gunman dropped toward the ground, a massive right arm stopped him as an equally strong left hand reached for the second assailant. Grabbing the second assailant by the small of his neck and with a mighty pull, the doorman smashed the two assailants together with such force they were knocked unconscious. Then he let two robbers drop to the asphalt.

"Mr. Will are you OK?" the doorman asked. "And you, ma'am?"

Both assured the doorman that they were fine although shaken up. With a sense of relief, the young man and his date hugged, then turned their focus back to their hero, the massive Nigerian doorman. Standing well over 6 feet, his curiosity and attention to detail had saved the couple.

"Thanks, Ado. That was pretty impressive," Will offered.

"But, you two are all right?"

"Yeah, just nervous," answered Will. "Are you OK?"

The doorman brushed the suggestion off. He was after all, the hero of the hour. He looked down at the two comatose punks on the asphalt. "Stupid kids. Stupid . . ."

Will turned his attention to his female companion, she had been forgotten once the action began. "Are you, OK?"

"Yes, but what in the hell was that deaf act about? You should have just given them your wallet."

"I was buying time," Will said.

The street began to fill with gawkers and then police. Will motioned to Ado that they were heading back to the restaurant. "I need a drink."

Not willing to let it go, his female friend demanded, "Why did you act deaf?"

"Look, I told you. I needed to buy some time," Will explained. "We needed help. . . . Besides, once Charles got out of a speeding ticket back in college acting deaf," he said. "It was pretty funny. It worked, but now, we really need to get out of here."

"Charles. That figures," she said. "But, this was not a speeding ticket. They had a gun!"

"You sound like my Dad—"

"Sir, we're gonna need a statement from you," a Dallas police officer interrupted.

With a fake smile and turning to his friend, Will sarcastically offered an insincere reply. "Thanks for nothing. I was trying to avoid this. My family doesn't like publicity."

As he turned to walk away with the police, she offered a slight praise, "You're pretty slick, William Hoke."

The Slackers

Will made his way to the high-rise condo in Dallas where he lives near downtown. It's an above-average loft that underscored he is, or has a close reach to things in life that most working stiffs will never have. He shares these quarters with his closest friend since junior high, Robert Grissom, who took the same five years to get through SMU. They both come from affluence and their families expect them to be more than lazy trust-fund kids, but neither appears to be in a hurry to grow up.

In their mid-twenties, they live their lives to the fullest. As single men, they devote themselves to leisure in sports, relationships and nightlife. Life is good, but Will had just been reminded by his father that he demands more of him than he is seeing. He is, in his father's words, a disappointment.

Born to a family of means, politically-connected and marrying right kept his father in the right circles. A man of little humor but a brilliant strategic mind to stay one step ahead and he was gold. With an innate ability to be ahead of the curve, Will Sr. had managed to stay relevant on both political sides. His father was the silent, yet sought after counsel people came to before they announced their candidacy and he loved it. But, Will? He never seemed to take to the firebrand drive of his father.

Too easy going, too relaxed and too soft. His father's namesake. His father's frustration.

Whereas Will was the leader of his group, Robert was the follower. A fiercely loyal companion who many had assumed were brothers, both had the same look, height and mannerism. It was Will who convinced him to stay in Dallas and go to SMU. Robert had already been accepted to a school in the East, but Will simply said stay and that was all the convincing he needed.

Along with Robert his circle of friends are Stu Sewell and Charles Bay. They also come from similar affluence, but they chose different paths in higher education retreating to competing schools. Much to their parents dismay they chose public schools trying to distance themselves from the days at Highland Park High School and all the pressure that came with their family names.

Will admired their "rebellion" and wished he could have done that. Charles had chosen the University of Texas and Stu had broken family ranks and chosen the rival Texas A&M. It was an odd choice mainly for Stu in fact, many would have guessed they would have made the exact opposite choice based on their personalities. Both made it out in four years but a grim economy brought them back to Dallas, but neither seemed to be in a rush to become the successful men their fathers were.

Stu could trace his family back to the Mayflower when George Soule, his 12th great-grandfather landed on Plymouth Rock in 1620. He was a true blueblood whose family came to Texas in 1838. "Blue Stu" the kids used to call him in elementary school. Although smaller in size, he didn't carry a small dog mentality. His senior year at Highland Park, he was voted Homecoming King. His girlfriend? She was Homecoming queen.

Charles was a similar story, tracing family back to colonial times in Pennsylvania. In Dallas, knowing things like this helps to separate the new money from the old and justifies the wealth bestowed upon them.

Tall and strong, he was the athlete of the bunch. He probably could have played at the college level like his father, but that was a shadow he no longer wanted to live in. His father called him weak.

Like Will and Robert, more is expected of him.

Will could not escape the most recent memory of his father's look of disgust. He knew he pretty much made his bed with his grades and law school was probably not going to happen. His father was in the inner circle of Dallas politics and knew all the right people. A major player with the Dallas Citizens Council, but sooner or later he would demand Will enroll. He had been doing legal work for a major firm in Dallas. It was only a matter of time before it was enroll or get a job.

To Will, in his perfect world, he would oversee that small Mexican villages get electricity and running water or maybe help aid famine-riddled children in Africa, not that he was a bleeding-heart, but it was just—easier, and it was a good thing to do.

He had once read about a Mexican distance runner who used his prize money from the New York City Marathon to fund a project in his hometown. Bringing electricity to a small town in Coahuila was an honorable deed.

However, heading a foundation was for the *wives* of CEOs or people of "lesser acclaim" his father once said, "People ask us Hokes for money, Hokes don't ask others for money."

This was about the same time he began dating Karina back at SMU. She was a poor girl from the Texas Valley. A second generation American of Mexican descent, she had earned a full ride to SMU on a Bush Administration initiative. She was a stunner. They began dating their sophomore year and it was then that Will agreed to go to Zacatecas to help with an SMU funded building project. He had 3 years of Spanish and Karina was going, that was all the reason he needed. Sure there were starving kids and all, but it would be a good break anyway.

He fell hard for her. He adored her.

Will knew they came from different worlds but he saw something in her, once confiding to Robert that he could see her someday overshadowing him. He was smitten beyond words.

He would often recall the first time they flew to McAllen so that Will could meet her family, Karina was as nervous as Will was relaxed. He thought her mother would take to him and it would be her proud father he would have to win over. Miscalculation. Within the first moments, he knew that her mother was not what she had envisioned. She appeared resentful and her aunts were no better, unaware that he spoke Spanish he wondered how such vocabulary could come from a woman who so proudly displayed religious artwork throughout her home. His smiles were greeted with a faint attempt of politeness then more words to the aunts who nodded in agreement.

He reminded himself that he loved Karina and he would someday win her mother over. He even laughed to himself about a movie they had watched about a white guy and a Mexican girl romance. He reminded himself that it was a comedy. He and Karina used to laugh at that movie during late nights. Yeah, this wasn't any different.

On the other hand, it was her father who embraced him. He noticed the men with him and assumed that they were Karina's uncles and family. Most had a look that gave Will a sense of unease. He wondered if this openness was an attempt to gain favor or to lull him to a false sense of security.

Speaking English with a thick accent, her father smiled and asked many questions without allowing Will to answer. It was then that Will dropped the bomb on her father. Will responded in Spanish. This caught the old man off guard and for a second Will feared he might have been presumptuous and insulting.

"Ah. *Hablas Espanol*?" he grinned.

Will answered back that he did indeed speak Spanish and looked for opportunities to perfect it.

"So you date my daughter to work on your Spanish?" he laughed and looked back at the men who were now smiling that the gringo was being tested. They were enjoying this turn in events.

"No, no," assured Will. "And I tell you that every guy on campus hates me for it."

"Hate you?"

"Yes," admitted Will. "Let's face it. Karina is a very beautiful woman. I knew she was beautiful but, I watched her many times at school and she always turned the other guys down. Finally, I got my nerve up to introduce myself. We went with the school to help build a church in Zacatecas. Lucky me."

"Well, you know we are very proud of our daughter."

"Yes, I know. She is also very proud of her family," Will offered. "But she says I will have to pass the grandmother test, but only if I pass yours."

"Ah, yes. My mother. Karina's grandmother," he said reflecting on his cherished mother, then laughed. "She might be the tough one."

Will was confused and didn't know whether to laugh or worry. So he laughed and added, "She also tells me you have a shotgun."

"Yes I do Will, and I am a very good shot."

The old man let out a big laugh and slapped Will' back. He motioned to the other men to follow. "Let's go see what the women have cooked. I'm hungry."

Will grinned and stood there for a second. He passed and he was pleased.

Times like this Will could often recall. It was his escape to happier times.

The romance had lasted about a year and then Will's father began to have an issue with his son, his namesake, and how this might be viewed in his circles. She basically came from nothing, no money, no family name. Was Will her ticket?

On campus, Will was envied, maybe hated. All the frat boys at SMU knew her and at any other school she would have been homecoming queen, but SMU, like the city of Dallas, arrogance and pretense are not considered negative traits.

A year later, Will Sr. finally got his way. His son and the Latina were done. Their senior year she got engaged to another, married the next year and never attempted to enter grad school. It would be hard to do with a child on the way. Damn, Will resented his father for this loss.

***

Dallas is known for many things. It is home to one of the biggest economies in the world, Neiman Marcus, two major airports, beautiful people and a can-do attitude. Think big and do it. You can love it or hate it, either way, Dallas won't care. Dallas is about winning.

The most obvious winners are the famed Dallas Cowboys and, of course, the cheerleaders. Dubbed "America's Team," every sports newscast has a Dallas Cowboy report even in the off-season. For those lucky enough to wear the Blue & Silver, once a Cowboy, always a Cowboy and your way is paved. Many former Cowboys still live in Dallas basking in their glory years. Dallas loves its celebrities.

It was that Friday afternoon in 1963 when President Kennedy was shot on the streets of downtown Dallas that Dallas earned the nickname as "City of Hate." The NFL commissioner didn't even cancel the scheduled games that Sunday and a week later the Dallas Cowboys found themselves in New York City. They were booed as if they pulled that trigger, but the Dallas leaders threw their support behind the Cowboys even more, almost hiding behind them. The young Cowboy team began to grow into champions and the shame that Dallas might have had at losing a beloved president in their town was soon forgotten. The Cowboys brought a Super Bowl championship home. Then another and Dallas had a new identity: City of Champions.

By population, Dallas isn't the biggest city in Texas. That honor goes to Houston and despite the Houstonians looking up Interstate 45 to their more nouveau riche, flashy neighbors, Dallas prospered. The Dallas-area is home to 7 million people. This comes from their sister city to the west in Fort Worth and the various other cities that make up "The Metroplex." Never mind that the Dallas Cowboys don't even play in Dallas but each telecast the citizens of Arlington play second fiddle to Dallas. Attempts have been made to name it the Dallas/Fort Worth Metroplex but somehow it always ended up as Dallas. Once again, Dallas wins.

That same attitude exponentially resides in every home within the wealthy Dallas bubble called Highland Park. A community within the city limits of Dallas, with its own city limits, school system and police force. There it is expected, no demanded, that you be a winner. Go in shake hands and work with respect and integrity, and if that doesn't work, lie, cheat and steal, or simply screw someone over—just as long as you win.

The ultimate insult in Dallas business is an unreturned phone call to someone not in the "inner circle." Left dangling, a business can die with a non-response in a wait-them-out game. While the victim stands in ruin, Dallas just moves on never giving you a second thought. She is a calculating mistress who will take your last dollar to find a place with her millions.

Will knew what winners were, he was one. Well, he was born into the "lucky sperm" club. There would come a day when he would inherit from his grandfather and someday his own father, but he was expected to be like them.

When his great-great-great-great grandfather came to Texas in 1848, he had only what he could fit into his wagon. Settling north of Houston, he bought 3,000 acres of land in Montgomery County. In 1888, he told his eldest son to move to Dallas. It was to be the new city of opportunity. Man, was he right.

If money was no object, and it certainly wasn't, Will could be his own man but he needed to escape his father and *his* money.

He needed a way out of his father's shadow and control.

Lunch is on Me

With an unusually warm February day, Will and Charles had just finished 18 rounds of golf. Although they were the youngest golfers on the course today, by at least 15 years, they belonged. Both families were members of the prestigious Dallas Country Club where membership is, invitation only. It the oldest course in Dallas. Their families had been members since its inception. Saddled right in the middle of the million dollar homes of Highland Park, it is a must in Dallas circles that one be a member.

Pulling his club out for one last inspection, Charles eyed his new *big dog.* "Man, I really like this driver Dad got me for Christmas," he said. "I drove 300 yards easily, maybe a dozen times."

"You were nailing them," Will politely offered. "Did you text Stu?"

"Yeah. They are already there. I said we were on our way."

As he walked the parking lot, Charles remembered it was the first of the month. Today, meant something. He fumbled around for his keys, found them, then called out to Will to come ride with him.

"I probably should take my own car," Will protested.

"Well, I need you here," Charles insisted. "By the way, you got $100 on you? I need it."

"Just use plastic."

"No, I need to make a stop first," Charles insisted. "I need cash."

"OK, but you gotta bring me back for my car." Will handed Charles a single $100 bill. "Why do you—"

"Hold on." Charles interrupted, as he answered his phone. "Yes, on Beverly Drive. Yes . . . no, east of Preston. . . . It's a white car."

Seeing a young Hispanic woman in distress, Will finally caught on.

"Oh no, you didn't," Will protested. "This isn't fair."

"Haaaa!" Charles taunted, "and I might need you in a minute for more help."

"No! Don't count on me. No way."

The SUV pulled in behind the woman's car. "Wait a sec." Charles slipped out of his SUV and approached the young woman. He motioned that all was OK and bent over and looked at the engine. Will knowing that Charles knew nothing about engines. His laughter continued until the tow truck caught his eye, then Will just shook his head.

Casting something between a grin and a smirk, he audibly voiced to no one but himself, "No. I am not helping."

The tow truck pulled up and the driver got out and assessed the situation. Will could see them nod in agreement, his semi-grin became a full on smirk and he felt a sense of doom. He watched as Charles made yet another call. Charles winked at Will and laughed, then pointed his finger at Will and "pulled the trigger."

The car door opened and the woman retrieved a small boy, aged no older than three or four. "Crap!!" Will said. "What next? Her invalid mother?"

The young woman put the young boy on the grass by the curb and then reached back and pulled the car seat out with a much younger child strapped in. Will threw his hands into the air and gave a defeated laugh.

Just then, a shuttle van pulled up and Charles walked over and spoke with the driver. He pointed to the woman and the driver nodded in agreement. Charles then turned and handed the woman some money, shook her hand, and got back into his SUV.

"You are such a punk, dude," Will said. "And with my money . . . I lose."

"Yep. I win and I didn't even need your Spanish."

"Maybe. Maybe not," Will said. "But man, you had to have staged that. That is just too bizarre. What are the chances?"

"No. I saw her break down as we were finishing up."

"No way. You can't see through the shrubs at that hole."

"Yes, you can."

"Well, how did a tow truck get here so fast?"

"I pulled the info on my phone while you were putting, and had the tow truck guy call the shuttle when I saw the kids. They live over off Harry Hines. Eighty-five for the tow truck, and about Fifteen for the van."

"With my own $100 bill."

***

Arriving at the restaurant they made their way to the bar, Charles was still laughing as he took his seat next to Stu and Robert. Will was still having none of it.

"What's wrong?" asked Stu.

"Tell 'em, Will," mocked Charles.

"Man, you are really proud of yourself," said Will.

"What?" insisted Stu.

"Today is the first," Robert offered. "The contest."

"What contest?" asked a student who had stopped by the table for a brief chat.

"Oh, well the contest is a thing that Will here came up with. I guess it was the 'make us better people' award," said Stu. "We, umm, find a good deed to do then, do it and we decide each month whose was the best. Oh, and we can't spend over a hundred dollars to do it."

"That is so cool," the young coed said. "How do you know who won?"

"That's kinda the kicker," added Stu. "It's sort of on the honor system."

"Will's honor system," said Charles.

"Hey, I'm honorable!" exclaimed Will.

"Well, who wins today?" asked the coed.

"Well, it's not just for today. Today's vote decides the winner for the past year," explained Charles. "See, I have four wins, Robert has two, Stu has only one and Will here, has four, too. Today, decides the tie breaker."

"Unless, Robert or I win," Stu interjected. "Then you're both still tied."

"And just what was your deed for last month?" Charles challenged.

"I forgot to do one," Stu admitted while breaking into a laugh. It was infectious and soon the whole table broke into laughter.

"That's why you've only won once," Charles said.

"I did too," admitted Robert. "I totally forgot."

"So what's the point?" asked the coed. "What do you win?"

"We each threw in $500. The winner gets two grand," Robert explained.

"Actually, you really only get $1,500 because $500 was yours anyway," Will corrected.

"Man, you are so trying to ruin this moment for me," said Charles. "Admit it. It's just killing you."

"You haven't won yet!" said Will. "Plus guys, this was just too weird how all this happened."

"Then, you tell 'em."

"OK, we are leaving the club on our way here and Charles spots this woman in a broken down car. At the same moment, he gets a call and gives directions there on Beverly where she is. The tow truck shows up in no time, she has two little kids with her who couldn't ride in the tow truck and he has called a van to pick her up and take her wherever." Will continued pointing a finger of accusation. "Just too quick and convenient."

"I told you I saw her as we were finishing the last hole and found a tow truck on my phone. Now, he did get there pretty quick," admitted Charles. "But hey, that was her luck."

"But today is the first of the month. Does today count?" asked the coed.

"It's in the rules. Until we meet that day." Charles confirmed. "We are meeting now."

"Does sound a little fishy," Robert added.

"Oh!" shouted Will. "Plus, he asked me for $100 right as we were leaving the parking lot."

"That proves I didn't plan it," countered Charles. "I would have gotten money from the ATM in the clubhouse and I would have been screwed if you didn't have money."

"Well, that's pretty good, Charles," said Stu. "Will, it's between you and Charles. What was your big deed for the month?"

Now all eyes were on Will. After all, he had put up the biggest challenge to Charles with equal wins and questioning the legitimacy of the recent deed. It was even his contest. He had started.

"So? What did you do?" asked Stu.

Lowering his head, Will hesitated to answer. He thought and gave no answer, but it was the coed that broke the silence. "Will, what did you do?"

Looking up at the others, he grinned then threw his hands upwards admitting, "I forgot, too."

There was silence, then the table burst into laughter. Uncontrollable laughter. As tears welled up in his eyes, Charles was able to get out a strained, "You were busting my butt for nothing."

The only ones not in freeform hysteria were Will and the coed who offered, "That's too funny." She then joined the others in laughter.

"I just frickin' forgot."

"Oh, this hurts!" laughed Stu. "Chuck wins."

Handing an envelope to Charles, the group continued to attract stares from the other tables and the laughter was contagious. People didn't know why but it just was catching, all patrons could be seen with smiles. The mood of the bar was alive.

"That's too funny," Robert repeated wiping a tear from his eye. "I am exhausted."

As the laughter at the table began to die down it came to a sudden stop. Shadowing over Will was a figure he knew too well. The others sensed this lack of comfort and all laughter was suspended.

Looking up from the table, it was Charles who spoke up first, "Sir."

"Boys," the figure acknowledged and nodded to the coed. "I see how Wednesday afternoons are spent by the offspring of some certain families. I'm sure your fathers are so proud."

"What are you doing here? Slumming?" Will mumbled.

"No. I ah, have a meeting with the owner and we thought it would be better to meet after the lunch crowd was gone," the man said.

The man looked about the table at everyone. Although most continued to look down, focusing on their drinks, Will did manage to make some eye contact. The tension was obvious—even to the coed.

"How are you doing?" Stu piped in a vain attempt to change the direction of the awkwardness.

"Doing well, Stu. Doing well," he said. He stood there allowing the discomfort to fill the air forcing eye contact with those trying to avoid his gaze Finally, he spoke again, "Well, it's almost time for my meeting. I'm sure you boys will be finding your way in life soon, making those families that each of you represent, very proud." The man reached down to Will's plate and picked the last shrimp by the tail and ate it. "Well, you boys have a great day," he said, nodding again to the coed. "Oh and, umm, lunch, is on me. It probably was anyway."

As he walked away, only Will watched him leave the room. He watched as he shook hands with the owner of the restaurant and a range of emotions ran through his body.

"Wow, I was going to pick up lunch," said Charles. "But well, OK."

"You can after tonight's game," said Stu, who, like the rest, made all attempts to avoid mention of the awkward encounter, but it was the stunned coed who broke the ice.

"What an ass," she offered. "Who was that guy?"

No one answered. The presence of the figure may have left, but the unease remained. Robert looked up and offered a supportive smile to Will, but everyone else looked away.

Again, she asked, "Who was that?"

In a quiet defeated tone Will said, "That was my father."

The Search

As planned, the foursome hooked up for a Mavericks game. Their friendship had actually grown during the late '90s when the basketball franchise was the laughing stock of the NBA and seats were aplenty. Never mind their families had season tickets. Empty seats allowed for the choosing of seats—to move closer to friends or make new ones. Now with a few winning seasons and the seats were filled and it was the in place to be. Constant reminders of their shortcomings were provided by former high school friends who were in attendance. These were the same guys they used to pal around with, played sports with, drank beer with, but now these same guys were joining law firms, finishing masters degrees or buying big homes—not living in an apartment. Basically, they were getting a life.

After the game, they planned to meet up the street at an eatery a family friend owned. They would always get a small back room table and would be able to spot any and all of the beautiful women Dallas is world famous for. Here they talk about those women, old times, sports and, the future. Here they are honest and remain accountable to each other.

Usually the life of the party, tonight, Will was more reserved. He explained that his father's criticisms were growing harder to ignore. He had always been smart. An IQ of 136 got him a Mensa membership. He didn't actually care that he was a Mensa member unless one of his better accomplished friends couldn't join. Will was a numbers guy. He would sit during a Mavericks game and figure if the attendance of 20,000+ paid just $10 to get into the event (his event) that would be a $200,000 gate! If they paid $25, then it would be a half million gate. Yes, he was a numbers guy and those, he thought, are numbers he could deal with.

"I am not going to law school!" Will announced, breaking his silence.

"Umm, OK Will," offered Charles. He also appeared to be mocking him as if his word would offer a way out. "Just don't go."

"Seriously. I mean it," said Will.

"Hey man, let it go," said Robert. "Focus that on your dad, not us."

"Yeah, but I've got to do something," said Will.

"What if you did have your own event?" Stu asked. "What would appeal to the masses, yet would not have much of a start up cost? A sports event? A concert? A festival?"

Charles joked that he used to get letters from the Reader's Digest people telling him he was "guaranteed a chance" to win millions.

Will gave a short laugh . . . then realized that was it . . . A chance! A chance which would appeal to people's greed. "What kind of chance appeals to peoples greed for money?"

"The lottery is already taken by the State of Texas," Charles said.

"There's gotta be something," said Will.

He watched the bartender line up and pour shots and it came to him. It was so simple, it was criminal. He drifted away in thought, then grinned that smirk his friends knew so well.

"What are you thinking, Will?" asked Stu.

Testing the waters, Will asked his buddies, "What if we did have an online lottery?"

"Oh, like those lotteries that spam your email?" Charles dismissed.

"No. This would be a legit lottery, but done in a way that people could actually see it work. The very idea plays to people's greed and something for nothing. In this case, an internet lottery or, better yet, a *raffle* that guarantees a winner. Each *pot* would fill up as tickets are bought. When a *pot* reaches a million dollars or so, a winner is drawn. Whether you buy one ticket or a thousand, the chances do not depend on numbers that you chose, but simply the *ticket* that is drawn. The transaction takes place via the internet and can be played from anywhere in the world. Better yet, it could be viewed worldwide.

"See, just look at the bartender who is lining up the eight or so shot glasses. As he fills each one, he simply moves to the next glass as people reach for the full ones."

Will explained that with a possible 3 billion people who could play, the odds were great even if we just equaled what the Texas lottery does. "They do about four billion tickets a year I once read," He added.

"We are *the house* and keep 8 percent of the million dollars. That's a quarter billion a year!

"Here's the kicker; the taxes are purely the responsibility of the winner, but can be wired to tax friendly places like the Cayman Islands or Switzerland. After all, it is the stealth of the internet," Will said, as he leaned back in his chair.

Robert understood the numbers, but he was critical, "How could we guarantee no taxes, better yet, the government would shut our website down so fast once they traced us—"

"The plan is to take the game to international waters," Will cut him off. "A boat, no better yet an offshore oil rig! They can't tax us. And who at this table has an offshore rig?"

Everyone looked at Charles who offered he did not own a rig.

"Yeah, but your grandfather does," said Stu.

Although Texas had enjoyed boom times for decades with oil, the 1990s experienced a sharp drop, and many of the independents were left holding the bag and today many owned rigs in the Gulf but global uncertainties and finances guaranteed they would stay unmanned with no plans for the near future. These offshore platforms had provided living quarters to rig workers and came equipped with satellites and phone equipment, why they even had helipads. The rigs were basically cities at sea.

The foursome debated more on the feasibility, possibilities and the legality of it all. Will just asked them to keep the numbers running through their minds.

Will explained that they would pool their money but to figure just what they could afford to lose. No one wanted to lose their trust fund but figured if they stayed under the radar of their folks no one would be the wiser. A simple call from a banker friend to their parents could ruin it all. Or at least, make them explain. Worse yet, it would keep them under their father's thumb.

Ironically, it was Will who subtly pushed the reminder that, here in their mid-twenties, each was still under the watchful eye of their fathers. Fathers who were much better at showing what hard work could afford as opposed to getting to know their sons. Fathers who showed up late to their athletic events, yelled at frustration over a missed scoring opportunity and demanded to know why his son was being taken out of the game. "Not my son," *the* father would say.

Will became more animated and continued to take the lead. He had more to prove to his father—or was it himself.

He was now possessed to find a way to make this work.

He stood and announced, "We're going to Corpus this weekend. My treat."

***

Once in Corpus Christi, the foursome checked into the Omni. The others might have thought this a party trip, but Will explained that could come later.

"Guys," he announced. "We have an early wake up call. I've rented us a boat or helicopter. I find out which tomorrow."

"What? Aren't we fishing tomorrow?" asked Stu.

"Not quite," answered Will. "I kinda lied about that."

"Then what?" demanded Robert. "We're in Corpus. Let's go hit Water Street or the Surf Club."

"Guys," Will calmly stated, "I am very serious about this online lottery. You guys go with me tomorrow. Look at what I have figured out and by this time tomorrow, if you aren't on board, then forever I'll drop it with you."

***

The next morning they drove to the Corpus port and the guys spotted a helicopter but there was no one manning it. "I guess we're early," said Will.

"How far out are we going?" asked Charles.

They spotted a crusty old man sitting by the pier with pole in hand, fishing the shallow waters. Although he appeared to be in his sixties, he was a man of the sea. Even sitting, they could tell he was a big man who could probably whip all four of them while drinking a beer and not spill a drop. A man of many adventures and stories, a man's man.

While they awaited the pilot, the foursome ambled over to the pier and looked out into the Gulf. Standing near the man, Will looked out in wonder as if this were to be his destiny, his legacy.

"Boys," said the old man as they violated his space. He nodded approval and returned his focus to his line. He reached down and stroked the back of a small, ugly little dog, a mix of who-knows-what, but obviously it was his cherished companion.

Robert, in an effort not to ignore the man, offered a faint praise of the small mutt who sat so loyally at the old man's side. Such a small dog for such a tough, big man, he thought. He knelt down to get a close look at the pup and politely asked "How old is he? She?"

"She's two. I got her after my wife died. She's a tough little bugger. She keeps the cats away," the old man said in a deep baritone that did prove this mannish fellow was a true man with years of the sea. "I had to have someone to greet me when I come home."

"Sorry to hear about your wife," Robert said in an effort to offer a slight apology for bringing up a sad memory.

"Don't be," said the old fisherman. "This 'un here don't ever talk back to me. In fact, she don't even care if I bring another woman home like my wife did!" He burst out in a laugh only shared by himself. Robert and the rest just gave a weak smile.

In an effort to join in, Stu asked, "What's her name?"

The old man reached down and picked her up from the pier and placed her in his lap. He looked down at the four pound *beast* and said, "Precious."

Robert grunted and covered his face fearing his laughter might not sit too well with the fisherman. He was just making idle conversation, not wanting to insult him. Stu just stood there with a dumb look on his face not knowing what to say. Will turned his face away and snorted a silent laugh.

"Are any of you guys Will?" a voice asked, breaking the silent laughter.

"Yes, I'm Will," Will said as he stuck out his hand to greet the pilot.

"Well, I'm ready and I've got the copter on the other side over there," he said.

As they walked away with the pilot, Stu and Robert began to laugh out loud. Charles hadn't heard the conversation with the old man and wondered what the other two found so funny.

Once they were headed out into the Gulf, few words were offered. The reason being it was early, and no one knew what to ask.

Inside the cabin, Will checked his map and got his bearings. He was clearly in charge and eager to aid the pilot on the head-set. Finally, Stu demanded to know where Will was taking them.

"To Charles' grandfather's offshore rig," Will offered.

"And how would you know where that is?" Stu demanded.

"I went to see him on Thursday. He knows I've written for the paper before and I just asked him what was happening with his offshore rigs now that he's not using them. He showed me everything in his office. Never suspected a thing."

"How do you know?" challenged Stu. "Plus, you interned only one summer in college at a paper."

"Well, for now, just let me help find the rig," Will said.

Once at the rig, Will instructed the pilot to remain with the copter.

"So he named the dog *Precious*?" laughed Charles who had suddenly been brought up to speed on the encounter.

"Pay attention, guys," said Will.

Climbing onto the deck, the four began to walk about the rig. Will inspected the offices. It was dirtier than he expected. It never occurred to him that an oil rig might just have an abundance of oil and soot.

He found the sleeping quarters, the room smelled of sweat and more oil. He found the kitchen, showers and, more important, he continued molding his money making vision.

"Guys," he announced. "This can work. I'll spell it out. Just, just focus with me. We are 217 miles away from the United States. International waters, therefore, we are not bound by US laws, not even tax laws.

"Remember, my idea about the online lottery—"

"Crap! That's still on your mind? I just listened to amuse myself. It won't work!" Stu said.

Will snapped back, "Just shut up and listen? When done, if you're in, you're in.

"Actually, it's not even a lottery, more like a raffle, but unlike the lottery you don't have to have the pick any numbers. By paying a dollar each per ticket by a credit or debit card you have a chance to win, but you can pick how many tickets you want per raffle. When each raffle reaches one million, a new *pot* is added, and the winner is picked from the full *pot*. We will only focus on a $1 million jackpot. You can enter as many times as you want. If you buy 10 tickets, you have 10 chances at that million. Theoretically, you could buy 500,000 and increase your odds of doubling your money, but make no mistake. There will be a winner in each *pot*."

Will looked around to gauge their interest. . . . Nothing—

"I've done some research and in Texas alone almost 4 billion tickets are sold each year. Worldwide, almost 70 billion lottery tickets are sold!"

He paused again, still trying to gauge reaction.

"If we just do a percentage of that we could make hundreds of millions ourselves!"

"How do we make money?" Stu asked.

"OK, that's the point. We make money in two ways. We make a service charge off of every transaction whether they buy one ticket or a thousand tickets. That will cover any credit card fees and still make a dollar per transaction. If 50,000 people average 20 tickets, then we still make about $50K off each *pot*, but here's the kicker. We get a *house fee* of 8%.

"Eight percent of a million is $80,000!"

"How do we do this?" asked Charles.

"All on the internet. Live camera feed, they can see the pot build, they can see the winner's name so they see it all work and know it to be legit. It will almost be like a QVC channel for the lottery. All viewed on laptops, desktops and, even phones!

"When we get a winner, we wire the money to them however they want. The taxes are theirs to deal with."

"How do we get the word out?" Robert asked.

"Well, that part will be a challenge, but we all have contacts. I mean, Stu, your old girlfriend Amy is a TV reporter out in Nashville now. So is Ryan in Austin, although I might have to be his boyfriend for a day." Everyone gave a small laugh remembering Ryan, a friend from high school who came out their senior year at Highland Park and how everyone, but Will distanced themselves from him. Of course for his good deed, there were the rumors but Will was straight and the only guy who could have pulled it off.

“There are other avenues with sites like Facebook, Twitter, Pinterest, blogs, we could even hire a PR agency.”

“I get it,” said Robert.

“How do we stay under the radar? I mean, is this legal?” asked Stu.

“According to a lawyer friend, the IRS will eventually notice this and try to shut us down if we are in the states, but we would be here . . . so guys, if you’re on board—”

“Guys . . . I’m in,” said Robert. “This might be a big thing.”

Stu looked around and agreed, “I’ll give it a try.”

A reluctant Charles hunched his massive shoulders and gave a halfhearted, “I’ll give it a try.”

“Then men, this will be our home,” said Will.

The foursome looked upward at the massive structure.

***

Back on dry land, Will called his lawyer friends, television friends, basically all friends who could help him. (Remaining vague, he carefully plotted how he would put this scheme into action.) Some he trusted, others he just needed what they could provide him.

Will had been stung by the criticisms of his father over his lack of “ambition” he was rejuvenated. His mother had often tried to intervene, but sometimes he wondered if it wasn’t so much of a cliché, the overbearing father, the ineffective mom, troubled kid, but Will has not troubled. He just wasn’t his own man, but he sensed the brass ring might finally be within his reach.

His internal motivation grew as he would prove his father wrong. In some way, he would even prove Karina wrong. She never should have given up when Will broke it off.

The Planning

Back in Dallas, the foursome planned to meet with a friend of the families. He was a distinguished attorney, a former Bush appointee to the IRS, who came back to Texas after Bush's last term and used that leverage to become the Chairman of Baker & Stein (the world's largest law firm). His walls were full of the usual degrees, awards and the pre-requisite photos of those in power. Political aspirations of his own, Bob Patterson was the inner circle of Dallas politics and these boys are future products of the same circle. He could be their ally.

"Men, you look serious," Patterson declared as he greeted them and offered seats. "Enlighten me. We've got five minutes."

Will lead off with a serious tone. "Sir, first, umm, thanks for the last minute meeting, but we, I have this idea, that, umm might be in the gray area of the law. We need some guidance."

"You want me to help you break the law?" asked Patterson.

"No sir, we just need to know how we can play this card and we'd like to do this in a legit way—"

"Well, spit it out, Will," Patterson ordered.

Will looked back at Robert for support but his friend nodded back that this was *his* idea. Will continued, "We want to set up an internet lottery, really a raffle that guarantees a winner, offshore in the Gulf, in international waters."

"First, you got a boat? And second, it's illegal." Patterson laughed.

"No boat, but we have an oil rig."

"Is it a floater or fixed? You know, those rigs, they've sunk before."

"It's fixed, a jack-up rig. It's 200 plus miles out in the Gulf and it has housed a crew over one hundred people, showers, kitchen. It's like a small city at sea. In fact, this one is even solar powered, it's just been abandoned for—"

"Forget that. It's not legal. That's the bottom line," Patterson interrupted.

"Well, we don't plan to set up any part of the company in the States. We'll claim Panama as that base of operations for the online gambling, we'll have to set up internet and video streaming there and phones will be satellite or some voice over IP or an 800 number. Whatever the U.S. product, we'll find an international company that can do the same thing," he explained.

Patterson leaned forward and smirked. He pressed a button. "Janice, is my 10 o'clock here? Tell 'em to wait."

The guys relax and smiled at each other. Did this mean he would help?

"Not so fast, boys," Patterson continued. "I'm doing this only to talk some sense into you. Now, how serious are you all about this?"

"Sir," Will added, "look, I understand that you would not want to be sullied by this. I chose you because of discretion, for your time, name and our family's history, and perhaps you could point us to an attorney who would be willing to help, if you won't—"

"It wouldn't be worth it to anyone I know."

"Forget the world population of 7 billion people. The Texas State Lottery alone sold over 3.7 billion tickets last year. And at 8% that we keep as the *house*, we would make $296 million annually. That's over $500 a MINUTE!"

Patterson recoiled in disbelief at Will's sudden brash attitude.

Sensing his power, Will added, "And we'll make in 3 to 4 minutes what you make in an hour." It was then that Will realized he has spoken in error and maybe pushed too hard. Stu and Charles seize the "uh, oh" moment and attempted to thaw the ice, but froze themselves.

"Why, you little sh—" Patterson halted and carefully thought of his next words. The once powerful attorney produced a quick smile at his underestimated guest and replied, "You've spent some time on this, I see, but, bottom line you'll catch the attention of the government, the IRS, and possibly international taxing sources. I have no interest."

Charles was the first to stand and stuck out his hand to shake Patterson's. He thanked him for his time.

Everyone stood and shook hands and began to leave. Exiting the door, Patterson called out to Will, who stopped and turned back for his expected rebuke.

"Son, has your father ever seen that side of you before?" He continued before allowing Will to confirm or deny. "Maybe you should consider law school after all."

"Thank you, sir," Will said. Then turned back and added, "Attorney-client confidentiality, right?" Exiting with his trademark smirking grin.

Caught off-guard, Patterson agreed before realizing the reason he was chosen.

"Oh, my gosh. That was classic," Stu said, throwing his head back in laughter.

"I don't get it," Charles challenged. "He won't help."

"He'll help more than you know." Robert realized what just happened. "He's now in an awkward position. We're only talking about this, but he is now privy to it. If we pull this off, he knew so why didn't he tell. If he tells, he breaks attorney-client relations, plus if he ever runs for office . . ."

***

Once again, they were back at the American Airlines Center, this time for a Dallas Stars hockey game (their second home). Back before they had girlfriends, back when there were no musical chairs with family members to do the same games for all four buddies to sit together, tonight's "date night" was a guy's night.

Tonight was different because all four guys sat together while the girlfriends sat together. This was a little odd because attending games with girlfriends allowed the hall pass the guys sought but suddenly the guys seemed very secretive. The girls even made a couple of insinuating jokes to separate the boys. It didn't work. All Will wanted to do was to talk about their scheme, but the game, the people, the noise, it just wasn't going to happen.

"Guys, can we all get free tonight and meet up to talk?" Will asked.

"Nope. Not tonight," said Stu. "Hope is all on me about not spending enough time with her and quite frankly, what I got planned, you guys are not invited."

"Meet tomorrow morning?" asked Will.

Walking from the game, Hope began to press Stu on his whereabouts for the last couple of weeks. She accused him of seeing someone else. He deflected her charges and accusations that something was up.

"Look," Stu said, "I'm a little under the gun on something and I'm talking with the guys about an investment. That's all."

"What is it?"

"Can't say, but it might take some capital."

"Well, I know something is up with one of you guys. I know one of you is cheating. My guess is Will. So does Mary—I mean he's being even more weird lately, and how obvious was it that he was checking out the cheerleaders tonight."

"Hell, we all were," joked Stu, seeing his joke fell flat. "Hey, look, all's good." He tried to assure Hope (joking aside) he didn't want to blow it with her tonight.

The Run-Up

The next morning at a local breakfast spot, the guys sat relaxed. Will huddled himself over some papers and spoke to no one in particular. He stopped, then handed each a list with numbers and figures.

"Guys, here's everything we need to do, to buy, and to keep our stories straight for the duration." Will looked for a response then added, "This is our game plan."

The trio stared blankly at Will. It never occurred to them that they might be gone from home for long periods of time.

"Guys, it might be noticed that we'll be gone for weeks, months even. I mean, some of us will be in the States trying to get hits or attention to the site but we've got to get the world to see this as being legit. Let's face it, not a lot of trust instantly."

Stu asked, "Where are we going to claim to be and will our cell phones even reach 200 miles out of the States? By the way, Mary thinks you're cheating on her. Just saying."

Will continued, "Robert and I will *be* in Mexico doing the goodwill thing and helping the locals get electricity, running water, etc. Chuck and Stu, you are starting a fishing business in Corpus. Corpus is ideal since it's *close* to the rig and has an airport. We'll need international phones and I know, she thinks it's the new associate at the firm. I must confess, if I were to cheat, it would be with her."

Robert countered, "First, you did the mission thing 4 or 5 years ago. Mexico is a dangerous place now. I hear the cartels take Americans as hostages for ransom and why have I not seen this new associate at your firm?"

"I know. I was thinking the same thing," said Stu.

"I've seen her. Hot. I wished I'd seen her when we were both at UT," said Charles.

The guys all agreed and start talking about the hot associate.

Will interrupted the idle talk. "Guys . . . focus."

"Won't your family ask why you're going to Mexico?" asked Stu.

"We all need a break from each other. Oh, and guys, you know not to tell your girlfriends because, well seriously, hell hath no fury. . . . Remember Penélope Cruz's character in *Blow* when she told that cop that her husband had all that cocaine in the car?" Will reasoned.

"Umm, not real cool with you using that analogy with what we're doing there, Will," Stu said.

"Girls talk, OK?" offered Will. "Hey, anyone with a few too many drinks talks."

Charles is eyeing the paper and asked, "We're gonna need $60,000 for startup cost? Wow, twelve grand for computers alone, three for printers, bedding, webcams, boat rental? Helicopter rental?"

"It adds up fast," Will said

"Where are we getting *employees*? It sounds like we're gonna need some," asked Robert.

"Mexican day laborers to help clean up and install things that are broken, but finding the computer geeks to help install software and satellites is going to be the tricky part," said Will.

"Satellites?" questioned Stu.

"Yeah, the ones out there are the real big ones from, like the '80s. Now guys, I need 15 grand from each of you. But quick, I need to make a token appearance at the law firm," said Will.

"Can we come?" they asked in unison.

"What?"

"The hot new girl," said Stu.

The New Home

The next three weeks were devoted to ensuring all the proper amenities were up and working on the rig. Will found himself going back and forth between Dallas and the rig. He accounted for this travel as helping friends, checking out law schools, and a various assortment of lies.

It was late March and the rig was complete with computers, webcams, printers, phones and flat screen television sets. The living quarters could now house 20 or so, a couple of showers and even a small TV room between shifts for a dozen employees to hang out in between shifts. Will realized that they were starting out smaller than he planned, but the guys convinced him to hold back in case the idea didn't take off. He laughed when he thought about finding workers on Craigslist and convincing them to sign an affidavit of secrecy. The only way to enforce it would be to take them to court (if they ever talked) where he would have to admit to running a lottery, something that he obviously would not, could not, do.

He moved the planned launch date from April 15, an irony that was totally lost in his focus to begin, he had hit all the message boards, started fictions Facebook friends around the world. He launched the website MundoLottery.com thinking it was as global as he could get. *Mundo* (Spanish/Portuguese) or

Monde (French) and well, every country knew what a lottery was. Would the world understand that it was actually a raffle? If so, it meant a guaranteed winner.

The thought that he might need a bogus winner, just in case, came to mind—too risky, he thought.

When three hectic weeks of getting everything ready had finally passed, he was standing on the platform checking his watch, it read a few minutes after noon and no boat in site. It had been nine days since he last saw his partners, he wondered if anything could have gone wrong. Did they get lost? Did they somehow get detained? Could they trust the guy with the boat? They had told the captain that they were shooting documentaries and hoped that he understood the need for privacy. And they had paid him more than he requested. That should have bought his silence.

Finally, in the distance, he spotted the boat. As it drew closer, he ran to the helipad to get a better view. He could see Stu, Charles and Robert and about eight others that he didn't know.

He called out to an old man to come help, "*Ayudame! Ayudame*!" Jumping down, level by level, he came closer to the sea. The old man followed, trying to hurry, end though his advanced age slowed him, his excitement sustained him.

As the boat arrived at the dock, Will dialed back his emotions. Instead of his planned enthusiastic welcome, he offered a simple handshake to the newcomers. His partners looked at each other as if to acknowledge that his demeanor was odd and unfamiliar.

"Follow me," he said to the group. "We have an orientation planned for the morning, but tonight we eat and rest. We do have men's and women's living quarters. OK, everyone in the elevator."

***

That night, the group was on the open deck, overlooking the sea. It was all ocean and a full moon. It was a fun night, but not celebratory. Work was at hand and Will would try to keep everything on track.

He noticed one standout. She was gorgeous and her straight, brown hair reminded him of someone from his past. Someone his father did not approve and demanded he move on. He resented himself for being such a wimp. At least once, during their fights, he should have just hauled off and popped his father a good one. Believe it or not, a good right hook might have won his father's approval.

He opened his wallet and *she* was still there. Karina. He quietly compared them.

***

The next morning, eight groggy newcomers were awakened at 8 a.m. to begin the day.

"Breakfast until 8:55, then we meet on the third level at 9 sharp!" Charles barked.

"Up and at 'em!" Stu chimed in. "Two days 'til launch! Two days." He laughed that he never even considered the corps while at Texas A&M, and now he sounded like a drill sergeant.

Once everyone was seated for breakfast (a semi-self serve buffet) Robert addressed the group, "Guys." Pointing to the old Hispanic male, "this is Hector, and this is his wife Ramona. They will be our caretakers while we are here at Mundo Island. They are here to cook for us every day. They will do some laundry and clean up, but they are not, I repeat not, to be abused and to be at your beck and call. They are here to make life easier on us. Their English is so-so, you are better off if you speak in Spanish." The latter brought a laughter that broke the tension.

"As time goes on, we'll be better at knowing your needs and will work to facilitate them."

There were six males and only two females, amongst the newcomers, a fact that Stu pointed out to Charles. He even pointed out how one of the girls looked like, well, you know.

"Don't even go there," warned Robert, who had overheard their conversation, "and she doesn't look like her anyway."

"Yeah, then how did you know who I was talking about?" asked Stu, seeing his point was well taken.

When the 9 o'clock hour came, the group was ushered into an area with a whiteboard, table, and 8 shot glasses. They sat down and eyed their new surroundings. Will stepped up and began the orientation.

"Last year, lotteries throughout the world sold just under 200 billion. That's billion with a **B**. In Texas alone, almost 4 billion were sold. We're not a state but out here, miles away from the U.S., in international waters, we are one. Therefore, we can develop our own laws and lottery." He paused to let that sink in and to gauge their reaction. "However, we aren't a lottery. We are a raffle and unlike the lottery where you must have all correct numbers, a raffle has only one winner. One guaranteed winner. This is not a game of chance, precision *and* luck, it's only a game of luck. One lucky person walks away with the winning ticket."

He smiled that his presentation was so smooth. He sounded so academic.

"Any of you former bartenders?"

A couple of guys held up their hands, Will picked one.

"Name?"

"Trent."

"OK, Trent, the bartender. Pour me a row of shots with those glasses in front of you."

Trent grabbed the bottle of a liquid colored *something* and began to pour the first glass. As it neared the top—

"Stop!"

Trent looked back at Will, spilling some of the liquid.

"Trent, you just exhibited the first full million dollar jackpot." He looked around the room to see if his point was understood. "Continue, with the next ones, please."

Trent continued pouring into the second glass, slowing as it neared the top.

"Keep going."

Trent moved to the third glass.

"Now, we have just filled up the second million . . ." explained Will, "and now the third, fourth, fifth—you get the picture. When one *pot* is filled, we go to the next, but first, we pull a number from that *pot*, Bam!! You got your winner!"

"I get it," voiced a lanky guy wearing a Milli Vanilli T-shirt.

The others joined in and the foursome wondered if they really got the concept or they were faking it so as not to appear foolish.

"Also, we figure that approximately 70,000 people will play each *pot*. For every player that buys in lots of 100 or more, they get pulled from an additional $10,000, pulled out of the 8% the house keeps. If 200 are in the pot for that, we pull 5 numbers and have five winners at $2,000 apiece."

"Cool," *Milli Vanilli* offered.

"But then we're only clearing 7%," Charles leaned in and said in a hushed tone. "Who the hell decided this?"

"Back off," Will demanded. "I did more research on the number of people who will play and it is closer to 100,000, not 50,000. That's 20 grand more on service charges we make.

We'll gross $180,000 off each pot. One hundred and eighty grand!"

"Now we have different jobs for each of you, but you will switch so as not to get bored. We launch in two days so the rest of today we'll go over manning the phones, the computers, emails, blogging, the Facebook account, the Twitter account, everything," said Robert. Then, turning to Stu he whispered, "We're gonna need more women."

Stu shot back, "You lonely?"

"Yeah, but people want to talk to women when they call in for help, not dudes," Robert answered.

Will took the lead one last time. "Is this a good time to remind each of you that you have signed an ironclad confidentiality contract with us? Otherwise, it is a long swim back to dry land."

The group gave into nervous laughter.

How's Will

"What do you have planned this week?" she asked as she sat up in bed.

Though, in her mid-40's, the years had been kind to her. Bonnie Hoke, the mother of three was still someone who could make a man half her age take notice. Will always had an extra lift in his step when in public, and she was the one who saw a different side of him that he hid from the rest. With her, he was not the hard-assed father who hovered over his son, but rather an attentive and loving man.

"Oh, the usual," Will Sr. said while shutting down his laptop. "I do have to fly down to San Antonio on Wednesday. . . . Oh, and Friday I start playing in that weekend golfing tournament. Why do you ask?"

"Well, our anniversary is Friday and I thought we could get away," she said.

"I thought it was next month."

"Will, you know good and well it's in April. Don't try that with me again this year," she scolded. "You need some new material."

He laughed to himself. He did always try to fool her into believing that he had forgotten their anniversary or that he would be away on business but after twenty-seven years of marriage she knew the score. Will Sr. was a man of very little humor—and even worse at pretending—but it was a marriage that had worked.

"Bonnie, you kill me when I try to surprise you," he admitted in defeat.

"Honey, face it. You're no good at it."

"Well, in that case I can just cancel our dinner I had planned at McDonald's."

"I'm just waiting for the grand William Hoke production," she said. "I need to know what I'm packing for. Am I packing for fashion or packing for the tropics?"

"Bonnie Hoke, you are a presumptuous woman, I thought we could just stay at home and cuddle all day."

She began to laugh her soft infectious laugh that had drawn him to her thirty years before and she said, "Will, you are no cuddler."

"Well, I wouldn't know about that either. Usually I'm not awake to know."

"Oh, Will you are drawing this out and you are so bad at it," she declared with a smile she could not hide.

"OK! Fine," he said. "I'll end the drama and suspense."

He eased back off the bed and left the room. She reached for a magazine and began thumbing thru the pages.

"Here," he said as he dropped a few sheets of paper in her lap. "You happy now? No surprise, no crescendo."

"Honey, I'm just happy that we are doing something together," she said.

"Well, go ahead, see where your husband is taking you."

"See what?" she asked. "There are no tickets."

"Oh, yeah. Well, they are ticketless passes," he offered, "look on the confirmation sheet."

"New York! Will! I love it."

"And, we'll be staying at The Plaza."

"Oh, what a cliché, but I'll take it," she said. Will accepted the praise and gave a "my work here is done" gesture, and eased into bed.

"So I did good? Is the former Bonnie Brown happy?"

"Of course, I am. I've always been happy, Will. You know that, but one question, did you really get my sister to book these tickets for you? You couldn't have taken the five minutes and called it in yourself?"

"What are you talking about?" Will laughed.

"That's worse than having your secretary do it," she said. "Shame, Will."

Still laughing, Will asked again what she was referring to.

"I see my sister's name because she put it on Mark's card," she said. "Will, that's embarrassing."

"Hon, you need to learn how to read," Will countered. "Look, see my name? See your name? Your sister's name and then Mark's? This is because they are going with us."

"Are you serious?" she asked. "William Hoke, you've done it. You have surprised me."

"Well, good. The twenty-seventh time is the charm," he said. "Three kids later, a home tailor-made for you and a faithful husband, but it took me flying your sister and brother-in-law to New York to make you happy."

"Will, I told you I've always been happy. Now come here," she said as she pulled him close. "You did real good."

Will laid there with a look of total pride and contentment.

"You're enjoying this, aren't you?" she said.

"Yes, I am." Will confirmed then let out a small chuckle. "Mark, however? Maybe not so much come Friday."

"Why is that?" she asked.

"Because I only could guarantee three first class tickets. He's in coach," Will laughed.

"Oh, he'll be OK."

"I don't know. He's a big guy and those seats back in coach," Will said, smiling at the thought.

"I like you like this, fun but a little devious. Why aren't you more like this with the kids?"

"They are grown kids, Bonnie. I am their father. I'm not here to be their best friend."

"Oh, really?" she asked. "Remember when they were younger you used to be more playful with them. You and Will hardly speak now and when you do, I can feel the tension. He just hasn't found his way yet. Give him some time."

"Look, Bonnie. Chasing women and hanging out clubbing is not my idea of growing up. If he doesn't get serious with school or whatever, he'll be thirty soon. There is nothing sadder than those 30- and 40-something types who never grew up I don't want Will to end up like that. Chasing women in some Uptown bar at 35."

"You need to just call him up some time for lunch, for no reason. That would be nice."

"I just have such high hopes for Will. He's just pissing them away."

"When was the last time you saw him?"

Will Sr. just laid there staring at the ceiling. He waited for her to continue, but she remained silent. He tried waiting her out—

"OK, I'll call him tomorrow for lunch."

"You can't have lunch with him."

"Why not?"

"He's in Mexico."

"Mexico?"

"Yes, he and Robert went down there about three weeks ago. Seriously," she said sounding disgusted with his lack of contact with their son.

"What on earth are they doing down there?" he asked.

"They are helping to bring electricity to some small villages there. I didn't want him to go down there either but he was determined."

"For how long?"

"I'm not certain, but he emails me almost every day."

"Who's paying for all this?"

"Honey, I don't know," she said. "It is just a noble thing."

"Maybe, but what a risk," he said. "I just saw Robert's father. He didn't say a thing. Does he know? I did see Alton Bay the other day. He tells me that Charles is starting or buying a fishing business in Corpus."

"Yes, Stuart is buying it with him."

"Really? Charles is a big fella, but Stu, well, surely they aren't going to be on the boats," reasoned Will. "But anyways, good for them. Maybe Will can take notice."

"I thought you would know about those things."

"Honey, I can cast a rod and reel and hook a marlin but fishing with nets and boats and all, I know nothing," he said. "When we eat out, as long as the sea bass is cooked to my satisfaction I won't be sending it back."

"What are we doing for Jimmy next month? He finishes his masters courses. Have you given that any thought?"

"That was fast. We'll take him to dinner. How's that?"

"Really?" she scoffed.

"OK, we'll do something more," he said. "By the way is Cricket seeing anyone?"

"Why do you ask?"

"I saw her old boyfriend the other day. He asked about her, but I didn't know what to say. I told him to call her himself."

"Will, we have three great kids. Just keep the door open and spend time with them, especially your eldest when he gets back," she said.

"So, are you happy?"

"Yes, and you?"

"Of course, Bonnie," he assured. "Hey, at 46 you still float my boat."

"You just admitted you know nothing about boats."

"I said boat. I don't need to know anything about *boats*. There is only one boat in my ocean. You." He continued to lay there, smiling at his clever retort.

"You are such a lawyer," she said, shaking her head. "You twisted that one pretty quick."

"Yes, I did," he proudly agreed as he closed his eyes to sleep.

"Next year can we do Paris?" asked Bonnie.

"Of course. Paris, Texas it is."

Launch Day

It was 4:58 a.m. and all 12 were hunkered over a large computer monitor watching the clock tick towards the 5 a.m. launch time.

"Why 5 in the morning?" asked one of the new guys.

"Because it is noon in Europe," said Charles.

"Why does it matter that it is Europe?"

"Hey, it gives the illusion of a worldwide business."

In truth, the foursome were attempting to throw off any hint of location and in turn their own identities. They were in Panama, banking in the Caymans, with fake offices in Canada, Hungary, the Philippines, Australia and Macau. They covered all continents but stayed the hell away from the U.S.

"Is the camera on?" shouted Robert, adding. "Who's manning Facebook?

"We've been rehearsing this for weeks," scolded Will.

"I'm doing Twitter," Stu verified. "We've spammed every major entertainer in Europe, the U.S. and Brazil."

"Charles, are the phones working? What about the voice over IP phones? That's our only link to the U.S. and Canada."

"6, 5, 4, 3, 2, 1," the voices of unity resounded. "Launch! We have launched!"

The newcomers rejoiced and gave high fives, but the foursome remained stoic. It was their money and their risk. Looking out across the sea, they were looking to reach 7 billion people or some fraction, thereof.

"We already have 4,000 views on the site!!" Stu announced. "We've been up all of six minutes and getting close to 5,000 views."

"But, no buyers . . . not one damned buyer," countered Will.

"Well actually, sir, there are 200 tickets sold to thirteen buyers and it is now 5:11." Will turned to see the *other* girl speaking—funny he hadn't even noticed her due to the Karina lookalike.

"What did you say?" Will asked.

"I'm sorry, I didn't mean, sir," she turned around embarrassed and intimidated for speaking out.

"No, no, I'm sorry," he pleaded. "What were you saying?"

"Well, I see now that 212 tickets have been sold to 14 people, and—"

"What? There is no sound. Why is there no sound? We need sound!" Will demanded, directing his comments toward Stu.

Charles offered, "At that rate, we'll make the million in a week. That's not really a bad start—"

"Too slow. Way too slow," argued Will.

"I really think that people are leery and just waiting for some credibility," offered Robert. "Man, we've got to give it time."

"We really need someone on the mainland," said Robert.

"Five thousand people are looking at our site and only fourteen people buying?" he snapped. "That's one out of 400."

"We'll be fine, it will just take some time. C'mon, man. Time," offered Stu.

"I'm going back on the mainland," Will announced. "Back in two days."

"By yourself?" challenged Robert. "The hell you are."

Turning to the rest of the group, Will asked the girl manning the computers if there were any new tickets. Nothing. It was now 5:21 and only 200 tickets had been sold. This was a disaster.

"Just stay the course and do something on social media sites," Charles said.

"Besides, no one ever thought this would be an overnight success."

"He'll cool down," Robert assured the group. "Plus, the sun is barely—"

Frantically, Hector entered the room vying for Robert's attention.

"Not ready yet, Hector. We'll eat later."

"No, Robert. It's Mr. Will. He took the boat."

"Crap! Do we have radio contact with the boat?"

"We never took *our unit* out of the boat," admitted Stu. "He has both radios with him."

"Unbelievable," mumbled Robert.

***

For hours, the group watched the tickets slowly trickle in. Five here, ten there. It was like watching grass grow.

The remaining three began wondering what they were doing. What had they let Will talk them into? The lack of activity gave way to a somber tension.

"Dude, we are so screwed," one guy whispered to another. "We are not getting paid."

"What was that?" demanded Robert.

"Nothing."

***

A phone rang in the newsroom.

"Ryan Jensen, please."

"Ryan? He's busy right now. He's in the edit bay," the *gatekeeper* blocked.

"Well, I really need to speak with him—"

Cutting him off, the *gatekeeper* blocked Will yet again and offered to take a number, stating Ryan would call back just as soon as he could.

"OK, then. Just tell him I'll give the story to Channel 23, instead," Will responded. "Tell him that I was ready to talk."

"Who is this?" asked the *gatekeeper.*

"I've been indicted and—"

"Can you wait? I think I see him coming out of the bay." the *gatekeeper* waved at Ryan who had been at his desk all along.

"*Yeah, I bet you do,*" Will grumbled to himself.

Picking up the phone from across the room, a young man of Will's age said, "This is Ryan Jensen."

"Ryan, it's William Hoke from Highland Park."

"Will? Is everything OK?" Ryan asked, a bit confused since he rarely saw or talked to Will.

"Yes, everything is fine. I just need your help."

"Where are you calling me from? Mexico?" Ryan asked.

"Mexico?" Will thought to himself, "why would Ryan think I was in Mexico?" Then, remembering this was his own alibi for his disappearance to friends and family back in Dallas, Will said, "Oh, yeah sorta, but I'm in town and need to speak with you."

"You're in Austin? I just saw your Mom back in Dallas last week and she said you and Robert had gone to Mexico on some mission deal. I wouldn't go to Mexico now with all the cartels taking control of everything—"

"I need your help and discretion," Will interrupted.

"Discretion?" Ryan thought to himself. Now, it was Will who had covered for him back in high school when Ryan announced he was gay. As if being on the tennis team and the glee club had not made him a target already for the football team and the *popular crowd*, his coming out only guaranteed abuse. Will had remained a friend even after being questioned about his own sexuality. (Which was a stretch since Will's girlfriend his senior year ended up being the Baylor homecoming queen?) Will's overall popularity had been enough to stop the abuse. Ryan appreciated how even the jocks eventually accepted him—to a degree. His devotion to Will was solid.

"I have a live, on-air for the 6 o'clock at Barton Creek. You wanna meet at Threadgill's or Chuy's at 6:30?"

"No," Will answered. "No place public."

More intrigued, Ryan asked for his cell number and said he'd call after the news.

***

Robert looked out across the ocean and saw nothing but water. It was getting late.

"No word from Will?" asked Charles. He already knew the answer but just had to saying something. The silence was killing him.

"No, and I've sent a dozen messages to his phone and nothing," Robert said as he checked his phone again.

"Pretty crappy thing to just leave like that," offered one of the male workers. "If he were to get lost at sea, we're all pretty screwed. I mean, you guys made us sign that paper saying we couldn't tell anyone where we were going."

"Will you shut up? You weren't asked," snapped Robert.

"Just saying," he replied (well aware that he had overstepped his bounds).

There was tension in the room now. And they began to fear for their safety being out in the middle of the ocean, with no one, not even their families or friends knowing where they were. Were they even going to be paid? This all seemed so illegal. And who could they complain to if they weren't paid, they did, after all, sign agreements to come. Fear began to take overtake tension.

Something was not right but when and how would it end? They had at least nine more days before they could get off this hell hole—

"We just broke 1,000."

***

"Thanks for meeting with me so soon," Will said as he shook Ryan's hand.

"Please. We go way back," Ryan said. "Forget that I am Austin's most recognized reporter." He joked, but he still wondered what this sudden visit was all about. Was he coming out, too? Ryan couldn't help but notice the disheveled look that Will had and Ryan, well, he was as well tailored as if he had just raided the nearest Neiman's. "Will, what's on your mind?"

"Ryan, I know this guy who won the lottery but he can't claim it because he is here illegally. If he claims the money in Mexico, word will get out and he would be a marked man. He has no bank here in the U.S. to receive it here and he can't get to the Cayman Islands to claim it because he has no passport," explained Will.

"How much money are we talking?" asked Ryan.

"A million bucks."

"How did he win it? I mean, do the Caymans even have a lottery? You sure it's legit?"

"Well—"

Ryan's reporter instincts began kicking in and he stepped up his questioning. "Whoa, whoa, whoa, and why are you involved?"

"OK, coming clean time. I have just dumped over $100 grand into something and it is a disaster," Will admitted.

"Talk to me," Ryan said.

Will explained the operation and how the world population was to come make everyone fabulously wealthy, the secrecy, the offshore rig, the Caymans, everything. Ryan was both in awe of and worried about his friend. He wondered if he could help or how he could help.

After a few minutes, Ryan finally spoke up, "Your timing is great and I think I can help. Can you meet me tomorrow at the studio?"

"I'd rather not. You just said you were the most recognizable reporter in Austin."

"I might have stretched that one a little," confessed Ryan. "Plus, there this bitch at another station who is probably more popular. Don't worry after the morning news, it's really a dead time at the station. Better yet, just meet me in the morning and we'll drive in together."

Will stopped for a moment, thinking of how Ryan used to need him, and now the tables were turned and Will needed Ryan.

The Curious

A pair of eyes peered through a set of binoculars. Curious eyes that studied the abandoned structure that now appeared to be inhabited. Odd that he had not noticed this before.

A motion to slow the boat so he could get a better look. Then he dropped the binoculars, looked at his watch and turned to see if anyone was watching him from afar.

He pulled his glasses back up. The boat's driver asked, "*¿Qué piensas*?"

"*No se*," the man answered.

"*¿Hay que ir a ver*?" the other man motioned, asking if he should maneuver the boat toward the structure.

"*No*," answered the leader. "*No tenemos tiempo*."

The leader motioned the driver to go and the boat began to steer away from the structure, the leader continued looking in the direction of the rig. He was still curious.

From atop the fourth floor, Stu looked down and saw the boat pull away. He wondered who the passengers were and what they were doing.

"Who was it?" asked one of the workers.

"Couldn't tell. No flags and hardly looked like anyone was on board," Stu replied.

"Who else would be out here besides us?"

"Fishermen, maybe?"

"Didn't look like a fishing boat to me."

***

The next morning Will followed Ryan through the back lot of the television station, they entered the back door skipping the hassle of Will having to sign in and leaving a record of his visit. Once inside, Ryan motioned Will to go into an unoccupied room.

Taking a chair next to Will, Ryan turned his seat around and looked at him.

"After that BS of a story you started giving me yesterday, got me to thinking." Ryan looked very impressed with himself Will thought, a sort of cocky he didn't know he had but he was all ears to listen. "We are getting ready for sweeps last year and I did this story about these Mexicans who travel in all kinds of means to get across the U.S. and even Canada. I mean the immigration people actually caught some being transported in a truck carrying a load of Port-a-Johns. I guess they thought no agent would be willing to go open up a bunch of crappers, but they did! Found forty-seven men, women and children in thirty-two Port-a-Johns!"

Ryan laughs as he's telling the story while Will is uncomfortable where this story is going. "Anyway, I interviewed, like twenty of them and they are all very insistent that they be blacked out in the picture. I guess so they can try to come across again, but a lot of what they are saying is about coming to the U.S. for money, that it is like winning the lottery and so on. After all the interviews, this prick news editor here kills the story. I've still got all the footage. I just set up two cameras and rolled. I had a friend there and he gave me an idea of what they were saying but by the time I finished the interviews, the story was yanked."

He sat back to let the pitch set in with Will and sized him up. Then he added, "I can make a *news story* for you, just as if it ran here and you can upload it on YouTube."

"But, isn't that fairly unethical?" Will offered.

"Well, coming from a guy who is about to circumvent several U.S. and international laws? Pot . . . meet Kettle.

"Look, we shoot stories all the time that never air or get axed for some reason."

Will appeared to understand, after all, he had never been a newsman.

"One thing. You'll have to do the voiceovers. Don't worry, that's easy, we'll distort your voice."

Will nodded all the while wondering what he was getting himself into.

"Both voices. You have to be a translator in Spanish, but it doesn't matter because we'll bring their voices down after just a couple of words and use our own words. OK?"

"Fine, but I do speak Spanish," Will offered.

"Better. Let's get cracking," Ryan said.

***

The phone rang and Robert leaned in to answer. He noticed that it was the computer phone from the States. In his confused state, he skipped the proper "Mundo Lottery" protocol and simply answers with "Hello?"

"Robert? Is that you?" Will asked.

"Well, if you're asking if I'm the Robert in the middle of a big-ass ocean, stranded and pissed. If that's the one, then yeah, I am him."

"Look dude, I'm sorry. I think I just fixed our problem. I'll be out there tomorrow around noon. In the meantime, I'm going to send you a video link. I want only you, Stu and Charles to see this."

"Well, we're dying here. Nothing is happening. We have had 30,000 hits but only 1,800 tickets, so far."

"That's because people are skeptical. Once they see a winner, they will believe."

"At this rate, people won't care."

"Trust me. They will."

"One thing, when you come back, bring some booze. Lots of it."

"We said we weren't going to do that," Will replied.

"Look, either you're going to get a mutiny or it can be a celebration. You choose," challenged Robert.

"See you tomorrow," Will conceded.

***

Driving down Congress Avenue in south Austin, as Will crossed the Guadeloupe River he looked westward to catch the fading sun hide behind the Hill Country terrain. Soon, the bats would fly from beneath the bridge and darken the sky. Austin is legendary for music, Texas Longhorn football and now the bats.

He liked Austin. It's a fun town. He had even entertained going to UT. His father was no-nonsense about SMU. No SMU, pay for it yourself he was told. Maybe he should have called his father's bluff. Then again, he never would have met Karina. Exactly, he thought. He never would have met Karina and now he wished he hadn't.

Looking at his most recent actions: be it the level of laws he was about to bend or break, the hatred he was feeling for his father, his desire to win at all costs, the 9mm in his glove box, he wondered if he was still a good person.

Turning on Riverside, he pulled up to a BMW parked in the entrance of the Austin Convention center and rolled down his window. The person in the BMW slowly lowered the window and an extended arm handed Will a small case. A DVD case.

"I don't know what to say, I mean, I really owe you for this," said Will.

"You don't owe me jack," said Ryan.

"If this does what I think it will, your bosses will learn about this and you'll have some explaining to do. I'll back you up anyway I can."

"I know you will, and thanks," Ryan said. "I've already offered the story to the assignment desk, they said, 'no.' Besides, reporters get sold bad stories all the time and I can say there were contradictions with the story. Tonight, some things of mine will be *stolen* which covers me if this thing goes viral."

"Well, looks like you've got it all figured out there, Ryan. Still don't know what you're gonna want from me someday, 'cause, you know I'm not . . . gay."

"I know, but I've owed you for years."

Will glanced back at Ryan, "You owe me?"

"Will, when I came out, rather was outed, everyone distanced themselves from me. Guys I had known since the first grade began taunting me." Ryan's words were now quieter and almost hushed. "You acted as if nothing had ever changed. I know you took heat for it. I know you were labeled a fag, too. Yet, you just acted like nothing had changed when my whole world as I knew it had changed. You just were being Will. Will, you are a good person."

Breaking the tense moment and seeking comic relief, Will gave an awkward laugh, "Hey, maybe I was curious for a moment."

Ryan feigned no laugh, clenched his jaw and answered. "No, you weren't." He signaled for Will to listen and not talk by pointing his finger upward in front of his face, "and I owe you because, Will I was prepared to take my life that night. That night you called just to say 'chin up' . . . yeah, a *chin up* from you saved my life."

Will sat there stunned. He didn't remember making that call. He opened his mouth, but nothing came out.

Rolling his window up, Ryan offered, "See you around, Will." and drove off.

The thought that he had been so instrumental in a life that he had no clue about really hit Will hard. He thought of one of his favorite movies, one his Mother had made him watch as a child: Frank Capra's *It's a Wonderful Life* with Jimmy Stewart. That movie had always been a Christmas favorite of hers and each year she had the children watch it. She said it gave a great lesson. Will's father made sarcastic remarks about the silliness of it. Later in life, Will could not help but to be moved by the final scenes. He remembered a line in the movie when Clarence (the angel) tells George Bailey (played by Jimmy Stewart) that his life mattered.

He slowly drove back toward the University of Texas campus. He knew there would be a coffee shop with Wi-Fi and he needed to get to one so he could upload the video. It was closing in on 8 o'clock and he searched for the word Wi-Fi in the windows. Realizing that it was midday in Asia and early morning in Europe he could get some serious business once the video went live.

As Will pulled into a parking spot in front of a café he realized that he hadn't eaten all day. He asked for a corner table out of the way. He sat down and turned on his laptop. He waved off the waitress who attempted to take his order and plugged in his earphones.

He looked around to make certain he was up against the wall before firing up the DVD and then he waited for the video to load. He had yet to see the finished product. Ryan had a script that he had read. In fact, there were several rewrites and he had no idea what Ryan was thinking.

The video began and Will sat spellbound.

Two minutes later he started to grin and then to laugh. For the first time in two days, he allowed himself to breathe.

Going Viral

What had become a floating coffin and apparent failure folding right before their eyes, the offshore rig morale had become gloomy. Watching the numbers slowly jump in one digit increments was more than the crew could handle. Most of them had retreated to the TV room that came with the rig. Having stocked movies on the rig had offered some diversion due to the boredom. Then, someone found the fridge. The private fridge with the alcohol and a party was now onboard.

Will called the rig but got no answer. He checked the number and called again. There was not even an option to leave a voicemail. Obviously there were still kinks in their system. Will hit redial after each unanswered call.

Finally, there was an answer.

"Mondo Lottery," a male voice announced.

"It's Mundo Lottery and who is this?" demanded Will.

"Ben."

"Which one are you?" Will asked. "Why do I hear music?!"

"Ben, umm, *Milli Vanilli*," the voice answered.

"Get me one of the guys," Will demanded. *"What a dumbass,"* he thought. *"Mondo Lottery?"*

"Hello?" a familiar voice answered.

"Stu? Why is some dude answering the phone? We need women answering the phones," demanded Will.

"Will, we got a problem. We need you here."

"Just check your private emails, *only* you, Charles and Robert," Will instructed. "I'm in Austin but I'll fly to Corpus early in the morning. I'll take the boat back out there and I'll see you about noon or so. By the way, why do I hear loud music?"

"OK, but this is getting crazy," said Stu, frantically waving at someone to turn the music down. "We're just trying to up the morale."

"I know, but tonight maybe some time after midnight something might happen. Check the computers. Check your email."

Will hung up the phone. He wanted to go back to the café and check the numbers, but he was tired. It had only been 30 minutes since he uploaded the video. Too soon—he knew—no one trusted the site yet. Without a winner, people were just throwing money away.

***

Ryan stuck his head into the news programmer's office and made eye contact. "I shot an interview with a lottery winner who won like, a million dollars online but is having a hard time claiming it overseas. You interested?"

"What else about it?" the director asked.

"He's an illegal, has no bank to transfer funds."

"Not interested."

"No prob, but hey I'm missing some items since yesterday," Ryan confessed. "So, um, did someone go in my office? Like I said, I'm missing some things."

"Don't know," the director said, never looking up from his monitor.

"No biggie, I guess. No harm, no foul."

Ryan turned and walked away, grinning that he had covered himself should anyone see the lottery winner video.

***

Hector (the old man) and his wife, cleaned up the mess made by last night's party. A look of disgust was evident as they walked through the empty beer cans. Tripping on a wine bottle, Hector fell dropping the trash bag he was holding and watched the floor become littered again. He decided to come into the TV room when no one showed up for breakfast and to his surprise a bunch of drunken college kids were strewn throughout the room. Even more upsetting was it was evident that someone raided the main fridge and who knows what they ate. Supplies were tight away and not as if there is a grocery store a block away.

It was after 8 o'clock in the morning and he turned to his wife and motioned to just leave the room. Privileged kids, stupid kids.

***

Will stepped off the plane in Corpus and hurried through the airport. He spotted a shuttle van and asked to be taken to the beach.

"Can I see if there are more fares I can get?" the driver asked.

"How much to get downtown?" asked Will.

"Ten dollars flat fee."

"I'll borrow you for an hour for $100. $150 if I go a minute over," Will offered. "Deal?"

"Get in," the driver agreed.

Jumping in, he dialed the rig. Busy. Seeing his battery was low, he decided to save it for now.

***

Having finally awakened, Stu tried to brush off the cobwebs in his head. He saw only one other awake and asked if that were coffee he was drinking. Motioning towards the kitchen area, Stu stood up and stumbled, due to last night's bash, he slowly walked to the aroma that he hoped would clear his head. A feeling of guilt came over him. It was after all, his idea to raid the beer fridge. Their own private bar. He wondered if he did it to boost the morale of the workers or himself.

Inspecting the surroundings of last night's party, he went to inspect computers. It is then that he realized there is a problem. A big problem! Within an instant, Stu saw that the computers are all flashing. The screens have been hit by a bug or virus and he called out to Robert and Charles, who came come racing in.

"Something is big and something is bad!" Stu yelled. He sat down to *take control* of the situation. "Who did this? The U.S. government? The Panamanian government? The IRS? Hackers?"

Stu was frantic and kept repeating, "What do I do?"

Finally, Robert yelled, "Stop! Stop it! It says we have a winner."

"A winner? No way," argued Charles. "I wish, but something is wrong."

"No. It says we had a winner at 06:19:24 on April 18. And we already have $101,000 plus starting on the new jackpot!" Robert said.

Stu was in awe. "What happened? Is this a legit win?"

"Someone get hold of Will," demanded Charles. "He might have found a way to inflate the numbers." Charles looked around at the other two partners and warned, "I wouldn't get too excited, guys."

***

The phone continued to ring and with only two to six lines connected it was going from call to call for the workers, who had been roused into action from their drunken stupor. Everyone was now awake and busy answering emails, grabbing a phone line, monitoring social media, and updating the website. The crew had a lift in excitement but had no idea what was taking place.

Pandemonium ruled with Stu, Robert and Charles not able to verify if there was an actual winner or not. That would make them even more liable. Only Will knew and no one could reach him.

***

"That's all I can hold," Will declared. "You can take those last two cases." As Will paid the man in the shuttle van, he tried once again to reach the rig. Busy! His anger sped his resolve to return to the rig. It also worried him that his friends were so hard to contact. Within two to three minutes, his cell phone would be out of range and he had a five hour ride to the rig.

He tried one last time only to get yet another busy signal. Upset, he threw his phone into the glove box. As he eased through the harbor, he found an opening among the fishing boats and hit the throttle. He heard the disapproving shouts of the workers and other boaters as he lowered the shift and sped towards open ocean.

***

Since the boredom of last night turned into an impromptu drunk fest and suddenly, this morning had bitch-slapped everyone onboard into action. No one had taken time to check the old business email correspondence, nor had anyone bothered to check their personal emails. Robert finally needed a break from the tension and slipped into what was known as "the cave." It was off-limits to anyone but the foursome, but he just really needed to get away from the rest and chill.

He logged onto his laptop, Robert checked his emails and was surprised to see how many he had neglected to read. He had over 200 unread emails, but one caught his eye. It was from Will, with a video link, sent just last night. He clicked on it and watched.

Outside the cave, he could hear the commotion as the phone calls were being taken.

"Does anyone speak Russian?" He heard someone ask. "Can you email your concern through a translation on the internet to our address?"

"No, we are up and running but we had a small glitch but it is fixed now," explained another worker.

"We will be announcing the winner shortly, but only their country. It is our policy not to release names or even cities," another worker recited.

"*Si, Sì, questo è legittimo,*" said yet another worker as he attempted his use of Italian.

"Does anyone speak Hungarian? I think it is Hungarian," called out another worker.

Snapping his fingers to get their attention, Robert motioned to Stu and Charles to come into the cave. They followed and he turned the laptop around for them to view.

"This might explain a lot," said Robert.

The duo leaned in to view the screen, while Robert shut the door behind them.

"Watch this."

Ryan/Reporter: "A 26-year old immigrant worker from Monclova, Mexico has a unique problem, but he can't figure out how to cash in on the riches he is owed. For the sake of his security, we'll only show him in silhouette and call him Andres.

"You see, Andres is a new millionaire, all courtesy of a new online lottery called Mundo Lottery."

Andres: "*Yo fue hablando . . .*" (translation comes in over Andres) "I was talking to my girlfriend on the internet from a cafe in Monterey. While I was waiting to connect with her, there was a pop up from a website offering a million dollars to a guaranteed winner. I had a pre-paid VISA card I entered. I bought eight tickets. I thought little about it because I play the lottery in Mexico and the U.S. often and I have won some money before."

Reporter: "However, upon his arrival in South Texas, Andres checked his email and it was there that he realized that he was now a millionaire."

Andres: "*Yo no creo . . .*" (translation) "I could not believe it. I thought it was a joke, but I clicked the link. It said my money had been wired to an account in the Cayman Islands, but I have no passport to go to collect my winnings. I have no money to even fly there."

Reporter: "It was then when Andres contacted Austin News 4 for help."

Andres: "*No puedo* . . ." (translation) "I cannot receive the money in Mexico. There are too many people who might bring me harm or rob me of my winnings. My family is still there and I would fear their safety."

Reporter: "But, with no bank account here and being liable for any federal taxes due if he did receive it here in the U.S., Andres is in limbo.

"You see, this new site is not a lottery but rather a raffle. Therefore, a winner is declared because no matching numbers are needed. Only a ticket. And, since the site is operated at an undisclosed location somewhere in the world, complete with a webcam to watch the jackpot fill, there is little question of its legitimacy. The money is then wired to the bank of the winner's choosing."

Andres: "*Porque yo nunca* . . ." (translation) "Because, I had never played this game, I just clicked to wire the money to the Caymans. I really didn't give it much thought because I never imagined I would win."

Reporter: "We were able to contact the owner of the website and on condition of anonymity, he agreed to talk to us."

Will: (Voice altered and face obscured) "Once the jackpot fills, we have the number drawn from the pot and pick our winner. We contact the winner and arrange for them to collect their money. We, the house, retain 8% and wire the money wherever they request. Taxes are solely the responsibility of the winner but most people know of tax-friendly countries. Response has been incredible because, unlike a lottery, there is always a winner. The easiest game on the internet and we have made arrangements for him to collect his money."

Andres: "*Mi vida* . . . (translation) "My life will change, I can help my family and send my sisters to a university to better their lives."

Reporter: "Now not everyone will face the roadblocks in collecting their money like Andres. Most people have instant internet access, phone and bank accounts, and the owners have agreed to work with Andres in getting him his money. After all, this is their first winner and they want to make everyone happy.

"Ryan Jensen, Austin News 4, outside of Austin with a very wealthy young man."

"He got Ryan to do a bogus story?" Charles asked. "Unfreakingbelievable."

"I guess it worked," Stu offered. "He could lose his job if this they ever figure it out. We hadn't had a winner until four hours ago!"

"Not good, because whoever played Andres will eventually start talking," said Charles.

"What do you mean?" asked Robert.

"Hey, hello? I bet Will gave him a few hundred or even a thousand bucks to go along with this, eventually he'll see there is a lot more money to be made and try to extort from us," figured Charles.

"Look, we can't jump to conclusions and he did say he'd be here around noon," cautioned Robert. "I say in the meantime, let's just go into *stall mode*."

A knock at the door and one of the male workers stuck his head in to announce, "The second jackpot just hit $150,000."

"So?" asked Stu.

"Well, it's kinda strange because someone just bought 5,000 tickets in Bogata."

"Bogata?" asked Robert. "I don't know what to make of that . . . wait, check to make certain the card is not stolen."

"Already did," the worker answered. "Legit."

"Bogata . . . ?" Stu wondered.

Our Winner

The boat slowed down to enter the chute under the rig, he wondered why no one was coming to meet him as Will slipped inside the docking area. The rig looked deserted and he thought it odd. He had only been gone a little over 48 hours.

As he brought the boat to a stop and killed the engine, he turned around to see Hector standing there. It scared him.

"Hector!" he shouted. "Man, you scared me."

"Hey, Mister Will, glad you come back. These kids," he said shaking his head in judgement.

"What have they done?"

"Oh, they throw a party. Make a mess," he looked in the back of the boat only to see more booze and shook his head. "You get problems here," he warned pointing to the booze.

"Help me load this in the elevator," Will asked. "I also brought more food but it might be thawing."

Will rushed up to the fourth floor where everyone was located. As he walked in and accessed the room there was an eerie silence, since no one was sure what the mood would be and.

"Any word?" Will asked. "And thanks for not answering the phones."

"Yeah, can we talk?" Robert said motioning to the cave.

Once inside the room, Robert asked, "What have you and Ryan done?"

"Well, for one thing, we expecting to get more hits on the site. What are we up to now?" he asked.

"What's going on?" Robert asked. "Right now we are at 270,000 as of about thirty minutes ago."

"Is that all? Dammit, I would have guessed a little higher," said Will.

"What did you and Ryan do?" asked Stu. "Who did you get to be that Andres guy?"

"Who?" Will asked.

"The Mexican guy you got to be the first winner," said Charles.

"Oh, that—"

"You should know its only a matter of time before he starts talking and wanting more money," interrupted Charles.

"No, no, no. This works perfect," explained Will. "I did go to see Ryan in Austin. I know we've contacted the news outlets, but no one was doing stories on the site. That is why we had thousands of people come to the site, but only one out of twenty playing. We needed a winner. Once we had a winner we'd have a better chance of getting a real winner.

"We need *credibility* and with this fake winner, we pay out nothing. NO harm, NO foul. We just explain that there were some glitches so the rest of the world didn't see the jackpot fill up," he pleaded for understanding. "Look, we are already at 270,000 tickets sold and we are on a better pace than we were when I left here."

"So you didn't jack with the numbers on the jackpot?" asked Stu.

"No. I've been with Ryan for two days putting this together."

"Who was this Andres guy on the video?" asked Robert.

"He was an illegal immigrant that Ryan interviewed a year ago when they all got caught in Austin by coming in hollowed out carriers or something. They were all deported and he was one of the guys, that story wasn't even used in the newscast. It was perfect!" Will proclaimed. "I hired no one. The guy was all blacked out anyway and we dubbed everything. I was the translator in that video!! Our tracks are covered!"

"Crap," said Charles. "How many federal and state laws were broken here."

"So, wait," asked Stu, "if you didn't mess with the numbers, did we really just have our first million dollar jackpot?"

"I didn't mess with jack," said Will.

"Then . . . does he not know?" Stu asked.

"Know what?" Will asked.

"Our counter said we had a winner at 6-something this morning," Robert answered.

"And you wait until now to tell me?!" Will snapped.

"We didn't know, we couldn't reach you," Charles explained.

"We have our first million winner?" Will asked. "Guys, this is legit! WE HAVE OUR FIRST WINNER!!"

"Pull it!" said Robert.

Will pulled the numbered ticket from the system and matched up the ticket with the name. "Doug Storey from Flatts Village, Bermuda," he announced. "You are one lucky SOB!"

The Tide

The rest of April had sixteen more winners, well, *real* winners. The fake telecast went all over the world and got over four million hits. Word of mouth spread and they grossed over $18 million and paid out almost $16 million. They had recouped their $100,00 investment and had winners on every continent, except Africa.

They inflated the numbers of the visitors to the site and winners with additional comments. Appearance was everything. At least once a day and sometimes twice, they would have a new winner. They started to notice many of the same players returning.

After every winner, they would take six thumb drives and download the winner's number, name, location and the routing numbers to the bank in the Caymans. Each of them had a thumb drive and all were placed in a safe, locked and stored. One could say, *everything* centered around those thumb drives.

Robert found a helicopter, that they bought for a steal. (Nevermind that none of them could fly it but it was a good investment and could get them back to the states in no time.) They planned to list it as a "pay for flight" copter so as not to gain attention for themselves. To cover themselves, they would rent it out a couple of times a month to keep up that appearance.

It was the end of the month and Charles had gone back to the mainland to get a new crop of workers. It was time to send the old crew home.

"Hey, the new crew will be here within the hour and I want to thank each of you for helping us get launched. It was little slow at first but somehow, it worked," Will said. "I know we promised you at the end of the two-week time period that we would pay you the $1,500 for being part of this experiment."

Taking envelopes from Robert, he handed them out to the eight workers. "I know we said it would be $1,500 but like most startups, most don't make money the first year, much less the first two weeks. I hope this is not a surprise for you."

He could see this resentment in their eyes, but they had signed confidentiality forms and were miles away from dry land. What were they going to do?

The threesome gauged their faces and looked stoic, almost apologetic. The workers looked straight ahead. Each wanted to peak inside the envelope without appearing ungrateful.

"Did everyone get a bite to eat? Remember, you'll be in the water for a few hours," Stu said. "That is, unless you get sea sick."

Suddenly, one of the workers started making noises. It almost sounded like he was crying, the group looked behind them to see the commotion. An awkward snort and everyone turned to see *Milli Vanilli*, holding his money, displayed as a fan, it was more than $1,500. "Either, someone can't count or this is more than you said."

It was more money than most of the group had seen at once and joy replaced the apprehension they felt just seconds ago. Laughter filled the room and the threesome smiled acknowledging their surprise.

"Yeah, it's double what we said, but remember now, we've bought your silence," said Robert.

***

Word continued to catch on for the lottery. Each month it doubled, May brought $35 million dollars and by the month of August they grossed almost $300 million and netted $48 million! Projecting to surpass the half billion mark, they now were averaging over 400 winners a month! No taxes and all stashed in Cayman and Swiss banks. Some people had yet to collect their winnings leaving $16 million in limbo.

It was then that the foursome debated on giving interviews to the world media sources that had requested them. Will argued that it would exponentially build the coffers for all of them. Robert was leery, while Stu wanted an exit plan. Charles was the hold out, he wanted no attention and worried about the eventual fall out. They had had their fun, but fear and paranoia had begun to creep in.

"Look, we got a bump and have ridden it for a while, but now we need the legitimate world press to do just one story on us and then we will be even bigger!" Will announced.

"We're already big. Bigger than any of us ever thought," said Charles. "I say leave it as it is."

"We personally have over $60 million setting in various banks. Divided by four, that's pretty good," said Stu.

"What are we? Becoming our dads?" countered Charles. "Enough's enough."

"Robert, what are your thoughts, here?" asked Stu.

"Guys, we're making money like there is no tomorrow. It keeps doubling and we are willing to bail before we even plateau?" asked Robert. "Unless the feds get wind of us or we start to level off, I say continue."

"Do we have an exit strategy?" Charles asked. "I mean, how long can we ride this? If they ever find out who we are, we can be brought up on so many charges."

"What will make you happy?" asked Will. "I mean, give me a number. $20 million? $50 million?"

"What will make you happy?" Charles asked back knowing that Will was the leader and everyone needed to know what *he* wanted.

All eyes were now focused on Will. What would make him satisfied, they wondered. Will lowered his head and wondered how they would accept his answer. He looked at each of the three, debating even answering the question, then he said, "A billion, net," he watched their reactions, then added, "each."

Press Day

As usual, Will got his way and three of the four were now in George Town, the capital of the Cayman Islands. The trio had left Charles back on the rig. Someone had to be there at all times and since he didn't want to participate, it made sense. They checked into different hotels using false identities, all compliments of one of the banks.

***

"Ladies and gentlemen of the press, we are privileged to have the founders of the newest billion dollar website in gaming. Launched only this past April there have been over 6,000 winners with three, that's three people, winning the $1 million jackpot more than once!

"Never before has a gaming site had this much attention, this potential, and a *guaranteed* winner in every jackpot!

"Understanding the need for anonymity, due to safety and, perhaps tax issues, their identities are being concealed. You may refer to each founder by the color which is on the placard in front of them.

"For the sake of the world media and our Cayman hosts, this press conference will be conducted in English.

'Lastly, thank you very much for your attendance. Mundo Lottery understands that many of you have traveled long distances to be here and they thank you very much, so tonight, immediately after this press conference, Mundo Lottery invites you dine at the Ritz-Carlton's exclusive 7 Prime Cuts & Sunsets restaurant complete with open bar! So without further ado, I present you our featured guests tonight. Mundo Lottery!"

Having already taken their seats at the conference, the lights came on revealing three masked men (each acting a role well enough to fool their own mothers). Behind them, in lights, were the glowing letters that were beginning to captivate the world, "MundoLottery.com" and the cameras rolled.

In an almost unidentifiable British, or was it Australian, perhaps South African accent, Will/Red addressed the crowd. "Thank you for being here, my name is 'Red' and I will be the principal spokesman for Mundo Lottery. Many of you have been asking for months for an interview. Let's get started with questions. You with Sky News." Will/Red had this intoxicating feeling of power and control. He was the backbone of the operation and he enjoyed the attention. He turned to look at his cohorts, he could see their discomfort. What he felt as personal power, he saw their fear. Perhaps it was seeing the BBC, Le Monde, CNN, FOX, CNBC, a news outfit from China, the Wall Street Journal, Asahi Shimbun from Japan, the German tabloid Bild, and even Al Jazeera was there. There had to be eighty to one hundred media personnel in attendance.

"What is your previous work that would have you take such a bold risk to launch an international gaming site?" the reporter asked.

Will/Red froze for a second. He saw his friend, Ryan. What was he doing here? He could blow everything. Was he there to blow everything? Will tried to make eye contact to see if he could determine Ryan's mood. Then, with a wink and a "thumbs up," Ryan expressed that all was OK.

Continuing with his accent, Will/Red explained that he wanted to make it easier for people to take a chance and win money. Big money. He explained that he was a former bartender and the idea came to him while pouring tequila shots one night, moving from shot glass to shot glass as each filled up. But to get from an idea to a business, he needed advice so he turned to an acquaintance in Germany. Will/Red motioned to Stu/Blue.

Stu/Blue offered the phrase "*Vorsichtig sein was du sagst*," admonishing Will/Red for referring to his nationality.

Well played thought Will. Robert caught it, too. Home run, no wait . . . grand slam!

"Why all the secrecy?" asked a Hong Kong reporter. "What do you fear?"

"What do we fear? We fear that someone finds our identities. We fear someone finds our headquarters and brings harm to us or our workers. We fear that since we are located in an international area that is outside of all taxing agencies and international law that someone will try to make a law simply to put us out of business . . ." Will/Red said, realizing he was losing his cool (and giving too much away) he added, "I fear that ex-girlfriends might start calling me again since my new wealth might be making me appear more attractive."

Laughter broke out and the boys were back in charge.

"Let's just say that it is nice averaging a million dollars every two hours," boasted Stu/Blue.

The questions kept coming and it was clearly the boy's day. What was supposed to be a forty-five minute junket, turned into two hours. As it was coming to an end, Robert/Green offered an unexpected gift to the media. "Oh, by the way, as part of your media pass that we insisted you wear, please look inside the small envelope inside the cellophane. Each of you, whether you are a reporter, cameraman or waiter, have a $500 pre-paid Visa card. This is not a bribe. It only works by going to our site and playing the game. Your odds are 1 in 2,000 of winning a million."

The media was now in an excited frenzy. They could maintain their *integrity* and still discreetly play the game. After all, the cards only worked if they played the game. Red, Green and Blue had managed to reel them in. Feeling their anonymity maintained and mission accomplished, they relished being in good with the press, for tomorrow, the world media would become their PR agency.

The lights went down and the boys were gone.

***

The trio approached the helicopter from differnet directions. Once inside, the helicopter immediately lifted skyward, and they exchanged high-fives—the boys were pretty stoked. All in all, they did a good job. The main point was not to stumble. They had passed. They headed eastward, the plan was to eventually turn west and back to the rig, but first they flew the wrong way just in case anyone had followed them to the airport.

"Did you see that reporter from India?" Robert asked. "Whoa!"

"I was more into the reporter from France myself," Will acknowledged.

"The dude?" Stu laughed.

"No, the chick," Will defended. "Loved that accent."

"I thought the German guy was going to bust us when you spoke German," said Robert. "I saw the look on his face."

"Well, it only cost us $110,000. Money well spent."

The World Reacts

The foursome sat in the cave watching various world channels off the satellite—their illegal satellite. They missed the networks back home and the local sports channels. They really missed those sports channels. Back home, where they attended the games, usually in some of the best seats in the house. Now, they were watching it like the rest of the world.

With all the money rolling in, you would think that they would not resort to getting an illegal hook up off the satellites but at a bar in Corpus some guy was bragging how it could be done, and well, it did help keep the anonymity.

The TV wall in the cave had five 40 inch flat screens focused on the various media outlets that had made the trip. The guys watched the TVs with mute on, occasionally hitting the sound to catch the upcoming stories. There was one from a Hungarian channel that was not dubbed and they guys couldn't tell if it was a positive story or not. They were a little surprised to see a story running on Hungarian television although, maybe not so surprising since there had had over 20 winners from Hungary. It was a bit of an oddity given there are less than10 million people living there compared to the U.S. with forty-two winners, but a population in excess of 320 million.

They checked the jackpots to see if there was a bump in activity. Perhaps it was too early. It had only been four hours since the press conference and with the banquet immediately following, Will guessed their stories may not have been reported or even edited yet. (It was also possible that they were *spending* their $500 pre-paid Visa cards.) Flying back to their destinations, it had occurred that it might be days before the stories hit the airways. Will wondered if the banquet was even necessary. It had better have been. It was his idea.

"Whoa, here we go," announced Robert. "Ha. it's Telemundo."

"Shhh!" Will snapped—being the only one who spoke Spanish—he turned up the sound. He listened to the woman from Puerto Rico describe how she won a million in May. She explained how she got the money and knew she would have to pay taxes but at her age she didn't care. "I remember her!" shouted Will. "I kept telling her to go through the Cayman or Switzerland, but she didn't trust those banks—or us. Well, how do you like us now?"

He turned to the world atlas on the wall.

Charles had already gone to check the numbers.

"How many?" asked Stu.

"Three," said Charles. "We've only had three winners from Puerto Rico?"

"Then, this is what we need," said Robert.

"Got another one," said Stu. "FOX? I didn't even see them there."

They listened and gave high-fives, another positive review!

"Yeah, but it is still North America," said Will. "We need to be more global."

***

It was now after midnight and the foursome had retired to their rooms, save for Will, who, as usual, fell asleep in front of the two monitors on his desk. As he slept, little did he realize that somewhere in Australia a new day had begun. The top stories were that the prime minister will meet British officials in London today, an Aussie rugby player arrested for driving while intoxicated and, "could you use an extra million dollars? Well, then there is a new internet game for you."

The same report was running in New Zealand, Malaysia, even Fiji. Indonesian newspapers carried the story and websites in the Philippines and Japan reported the new cool place to win. In mainland China, a young man received a text about the site. The world was buzzing about MundoLottery.com. They had gone viral!

Will was still sleeping.

***

"Mr. Robert, Robert. Sorry to wake you but something is going on," said a timid voice from behind the door.

Waking up, Robert called back to the voice in the dark asking who she was and what she wanted.

"It's me, Mary," she whispered. "You need to see this."

"Why me? Is anyone else awake?"

"No, plus Will is asleep in the office and, to be honest, I'm a little scared of him."

"This had better be good."

It was just past 2:00 a.m. and only three employees were up working. "Well, what's the problem?" Robert asked.

"You tell us," said one worker who was known to be a smart-ass.

Robert squinted to see the screen and absorb the data.

"We've had eleven winners since I came on my shift. less than two hours ago," said Mary. "That's like one every ten minutes."

Blinking his eyes in an attempt to wake up, Robert asked, "Where are the winners located?"

"That's just it," answered Mary. "We have three in Japan, one in Taiwan, two in China, one each in New Zealand, Dominica, Australia, Luxembourg and Cook Island."

"Throw out Luxembourg and Dominica and you've got the Pacific nations— "

"Number 12!" announced the smartass.

"Where?" asked Robert.

"Louisville, Kentucky."

"Well, that doesn't fit the model but this is growing. It's working." Turning to Mary, he tells her to go wake up the other guys, but he'd wake up Will.

While the others were in the main room digesting this new *surge*, an awake Will stayed in the office studying the numbers. Sometimes he needed to be isolated and the others were happy to let him be alone.

"We have another winner," announced the smart ass. "Only eight minutes from the last winner!"

"Where are they from?" asked Robert.

"Wow," smart ass answered looking puzzled, "they are from the Caymans."

Visitors

Somewhere in Washington D.C., a young man sat at his desk. He belonged to the most feared initials in America: IRS. Entering his simple office is an elder, more senior member of the organization that had brought down Al Capone.

"What do you know of new online gaming in the U.S.?" he asked.

"Nothing new, sir. Just the usual ones that come into the radar."

"Well, I got a report that there are possible U.S. citizens cooperating with German nationals, possibly South Africans operating an online gaming site that could be in the Gulf of Mexico or possibly the Caribbean. Can you get on that?"

"Get me what you have, sir."

"All I have is on this Post-it note."

"Will do, sir."

All that was on the note was a single web site url: MundoLottery.com.

***

It was morning on the rig and Robert and Will were down by the boat, fishing. Not so much for the need to reduce finances, the money was rolling in, but for dealing with boredom and the prision like environment they were living in. Ever since the media blitz started two days ago, the world had caught on! They were now averaging fourteen winners an hour. The numbers were fanatical.

"Do you realize that at this rate we will do a billion plus for just this month alone?" an awed Will observed. "Doubt we will maintain though.

"And yet . . . I'm still lonely for a woman," laughed Robert.

"Seriously?" asked Will, puffing a fine Cuban cigar compliments of his visit to the Caymans. "We have outearned our families and you're only thinking of the women—such a dumbass."

"We come from money, Will. I mean, I won't inherit until my old man dies, but I've never hurt for anything."

"Same boat, my friend, but with my old man I never know if someday he'll just cut me off," Will surmised. "But now, I'll never have to live in that fear."

Pointing to the sea, Robert motioned that Will caught something. Will pulled to bring the fish in, a red snapper. Whether it was focus or fishing, neither noticed the small boat approaching from behind.

"Are we done yet?" asked Robert. "That's almost a dozen—Crap!"

Robert jumped first, Will followed. Both were startled.

"*Hola amigos!*" waved a tattooed man. "Sorry to scare you, my friends."

"Whoa! Where the hell did you come from?" shouted Robert, half-pissed, half-scared.

"Easy," mumbled Will to Robert.

"I have come by many times by here and see you. My name is Carlos. I fishing man," he smiled broadly.

"I didn't know we were competing," Will laughed.

Looking blank, Carlos answered, "I no understand."

Will tried again, "I did not mean to take your fish," and smiled for Carlos. They noticed a second man who did not smile sitting on the boat with Carlos.

"Oh! Yes. No, not all my fish. Big ocean," Carlos tried to joke back. "What do you work? You make the oil?" motioning towards the massive rig.

"Huh?" Will stammered still trying to access why Carlos and his companion were here. "Oh, umm, we are with a school, *Universidad*." Attempting to make a good story, he continued, "We work with the United States government to see if the oil makes it bad for the fish. To eat." He motioned an eating gesture. "We want the fish to be good for you, too."

"You here for long time?" Carlos asked.

"Two months, maybe more. We only talk to phone every night and we have no women. Very far from home." Again trying to make a joke.

"I see," he said looking around.

It was obvious he was checking the place out, Will and Robert looked at each other wondering what to do.

"We are getting low on food. That is why we are fishing. No supply for three more days," Will called out.

"I see," Carlos said. Then he turned to his companion and nodded. The boat fired up and began to back away from the rig. He waved to the guys and looked back up at the rig. "Best to you, *mis amigos*."

As the duo watched Carlos depart, they grabbed the fish and headed up to the floors above.

"What just happened?" Robert asked.

"Dunno," said Will, "but this is spooky."

"What the hell is a small boat like that doing this far out in the gulf?" Robert demanded. "And I didn't see any fishing gear there."

"Me neither."

As they neared the top, Will burst into the room where everyone was working. "Didn't anyone see the approaching boat?!" he yelled.

Everyone sat motionlessly. No one knew what he meant. Stu and Robert approached him and tried to calm him.

"What's going on?" Robert asked.

"We just had a visitor," explained Will.

"Scared the shit out of us," Robert added. "Said he was a fisherman. Will gave him some bullshit story about us being with a university."

"What?" asked Stu. "What did you tell him?"

"Well, we were caught off guard. I told him we were with a university to study 'oil in fish' and we reported to the U.S. government. I just told him that because students wouldn't be threatening but being with the government might be beneficial," Will explained. "I was playing both odds."

"Yeah, he was definitely checking this place out," said Robert. "Guys, he was in a small boat. Too small to be out here on its own."

"Then there must be a second boat," said Stu. "Gimme those binoculars and let's find him. Maybe there's another boat in the area."

"What do you think someone would want out here?" asked Robert.

"Hello!" mocked Will, "Could be drug runners out of Mexico or South America."

"Found him!" yelled Stu.

"Where is he?" asked Charles. "Do you see any others?"

"Yep, there is another boat. A much bigger boat."

"Just how big a boat?" asked Will.

"Umm, hard to judge against the size of the smaller boat but it's big," said Stu. "I see, a mast? Yeah, I see a mast and a lowered sail . . . you think they could just be a fishing boat?"

"Well, they saw us first," said Will. "And they made an effort to come check us out. Either way, this isn't good."

Now a Country

In a little over eight months Mundo Lottery had created almost 9,000 millionaires. What the world hadn't realized was that the founders had created some pretty serious wealth for themselves as well. In all, they had amassed a fortune of $1 billion. Individually, they were wealthier than all their families combined, and had been for some time now.

Overhead was so minimal, that they were "just printing money." Aside from the occasional helicopter pilot rentals and flights to Switzerland, it was pure profit. Even the $50,000 a month for the help and upkeep was a mere drop in the bucket.

Still trying to "fly under the radar," they even did buy a fishing boat so as not to attract attention when. Actually, they did attract some attention, as the worst commercial fishing boat in the Gulf. The other fishermen laughed when the boat would dock and the *crew* unloaded with no fish. Of course, the joke was on them, it was simply a ploy and the helicopter would always attract some attention, even in Corpus which had made its wealth on oil and cattle, so they needed the boat as well.

To battle anxiety, the boys had rented a home on Ocean Drive among the "old money" in town but quickly gave it up when the community reached out for fundraisers and political affiliations. The home was to be where they guys could individually slip away and escape the rig. Instead, they found a five bedroom home that was conveniently situated near a college campus and not surrounded by *money*.

On the rig, life could get cumbersome proving that money isn't everything. Relationships with girlfriends back in Dallas were now stagnant, even though there were the surprise trips to New York for getaway weekends and unusual gifts for no reason—but not enough to raise suspicions.

The ruse of working in small Mexican villages to bring joy and hope still worked. In fact, it was five months into the scheme of things before one of the guys remembered and sent $500,000 to get the small towns lit up. Their families were fearful due to the drug cartel influence in Mexico. They were thought fools to go. Good thing was, no one wanted to go visit them there.

Money changes people, but these guys always had money. They were the "lucky sperm" club. They were boys who would never *have* to work a day in their life, but were expected to. To them, money would just appear, but now, they were actually *working* and life was good. Charles wondered how much money was enough. If there was a weak link, it was him. Will and Robert had been the more laid back of the four, but Will had become increasingly rigid and demanding. He, along with Stu, had also become obsessed with firearms. Big, bad firearms. Firearms that can run six rounds per second thru the heated barrel of an AR-15, and Will was falling hard.

Charles was another story.

"Can you put the guns down," he said as he approached Will and Stu.

They looked at each other and set the guns aside and eased back to listen. He seemed so big they thought, yet he looked so insecure.

"Guys," he asked. "How much is enough?"

"Oh, no," moaned Stu. "This isn't about the money, is it?"

"Yes, it is!" snapped Charles, itemizing his argument, finger by finger. "We are wealthier than all our families combined! We each make almost two million dollars a day! We stand to make almost a billion dollars, this year—Each! Yet, we are relegated to taking up guns because we think that someone is watching us. We're paranoid."

"Whoa, Chuck," countered Stu. "Sounds like you're being paranoid. Who said anything about needing guns."

"Then, why suddenly are they so important? The only time we used to need them was when we went deer hunting in the fall."

"Just protection," shot Will. "Seriously, you never know . . . but seriously, what else is bothering you?"

After thinking for a second, Charles admits, "I want to go back to Dallas."

"We've been slipping in every month," said Stu. "You know we can't be away that long from here."

"Why the hell not?!" asked Charles.

"I'm not trusting these kids running our computers if we leave," said Stu, "they could wipe us out. If they accessed our accounts, business and personal, *they* would be the billionaires and we would be going back to Dallas without jack!"

"So we can't even trust the people we hire," reasoned Charles.

"Can we trust each other?" asked Will.

"What's that supposed to mean?"

"Well, you're freaking out, wanting to go home—why?"

"I've lost her," Charles fought back tears and reiterated, "I thought she was seeing someone else . . . and she is."

"Cindy?" Stu asked. "I don't think—"

"Look, she admitted. She's moved on. And, I'm done . . ."

"Dude, I never knew," said Stu. "I just thought you were just biding time . . . um, didn't know it was serious."

"That's why I never cheated on her when we went out," Charles admitted lowering his head. "I wanted it all for her and now, I've lost it all for me."

"Man, I really didn't know." Obviously uncomfortable, Will looked around grasping for words, "I dunno."

"Will," Charles asked, "what is our exit strategy? When are we calling it quits?"

"Working on it, Charles."

"I want out. I've got all the money I'll ever need and I'll double it in my lifetime but I have no family, no friends . . . no life here on this rig."

Will looked up realizing the possible mutiny and assured, "Give me a month. Just give me a month."

***

Somewhere in China, a middle-aged woman danced in her small quartered home. She shrieked her native tongue and hopped as high as her feeble legs allowed. She cried out of joy, lost her voice and let out an inaudible squeal.

Her husband entered the room and gave her a disgusted look. She approached him, but he retreated as if she is a crazy woman. She handed him a printed sheet of paper. He read it but didn't understand. She implored him to read it again. Her head repeatedly nodded. He read it again and began to understand. Normally he would be enraged by her playing such a foolish game, but he had a look of awe, even love, as he absorbed the full meaning of this paper. He danced. He kissed her. He too cried with joy.

The world's newest millionaires.

***

Back in Washington, the young associate poured over terabytes of data trying to learn the identity of anyone associated with Mundo Lottery. He looked at aerial surveillance photos and internet addresses. Some people had simply received their money upfront opting to pay all taxes owed the U.S. while others were content to allow their winnings to remain in Cayman and Swiss banks.

"What have you learned?" asked the IRS senior manager.

"Well, I have learned that . . . I'm still nowhere near where I need to be," the younger associate admitted. "I must say, in spite the possibility of at least one of them being a U.S. citizen, there have been no U.S. tax laws broken."

"That's not good enough," demanded the senior.

"I have contacted a couple of the winners who did report full earnings, with all the winnings being wired via the Caymans. One, I have just begun to investigate, informs me he has received money from Switzerland via UBS. However, he is claiming that the money was invested in Europe, thus, non-taxable since it wasn't earned in the U.S. We've sent a letter in hopes of *enticing* him to cooperate more."

"Andrews, well while you are waiting for him to cooperate, I am offering no answers to the Director," he said with a short smile.

The junior associate had been working for this manager for three years. He had lasted longer than another associate because soon he would have a family to support, so he was willing to put up with the occasional burst of ego thrown at him by his superior. Besides, he thought he could charm his way out of any conflict. A trait his wife said she fell for, but his superior was another story. An ambitious man, Andrews always smiled and obeyed.

"Well, unless the U.S. citizen does not report their income, file, or something else, it appears they have been rather genius in this endeavor."

"Son, admiration for citizens circumventing tax laws is not something we praise around here and could lead to termination," the senior subtly threatened. "This is not the sort of thing that we find even remotely amusing. Now I want you on a plane to Zurich tomorrow afternoon."

"Sir, my wife is due any day now—"

"Are you her doctor?" the senior asked. Getting nothing but silence, he continued, "Well, then. Call and book your flight. I'll give you instructions and see you when you return."

Calling Home

"Gentlemen," announced Will. "We all made a commitment to this and agreed that we might be away from our families and friends for a while but Charles got me thinking. It's coming up on Christmas and we *all* need to go home."

"Whew. Glad you said that," said Robert. "I've been getting a touch of cabin fever."

"Well, better than that. We fly back to Dallas, spend a few days there, catch up with some friends we've not seen in a while and they were off to LA for a few nights."

"What are we doing in LA?" asked Charles.

"Whatever we want," said Will. "I've got Lakers-Mavs tickets, a suite at the Nikko, private jet at Love Field and $100,000 to blow." He laid 10 bundles of 100s down to the table and looked at the other three for approval.

"This isn't what I'm talking about," said Charles. "You don't get it."

"No. I do get it," snapped Will. "I've been so focused on making this work that I forgot the little things. We've become prisoners here of the very thing we tried to avoid. From here on out, we will be free."

"Cool," allowed Robert. "What now?"

"We board the helicopter in the morning for Corpus, then, fly to Dallas."

"Wow. Pretty cool gift, Will. Is this our Christmas gift?" Stu joked.

"Wait'll you see what's in store when we get back," he whispered in Stu's ear. "Game changer."

***

"Welcome, Mr. Andrews. I am Matthias Geert," the banker greeted the young IRS associate. His heavy Swiss accent flowed and he led the young American down the hall of the institution, polite but cautious. "Your appearance was not fully explained on the phone, but we took measures to see you."

"Yes, thank you very much," he obliged. "This is very appreciated."

"You have bags? Luggage?"

Holding up his suitcase, Andrews answered, "Yes, I landed at 9:00 and came right here."

"Is this that urgent?"

"No, I was just in Customs longer than I had planned, so I have not even checked into my hotel yet."

"Is this your first time in Switzerland?"

"No. I was here to watch my brother compete about four years ago."

"To what competition do you refer?"

"My brother was on the U.S. Olympic team in track and field. I think you call it *athletisme*?" he said trying to sound international.

"Ah, yes. The *Leichtathletik* meeting."

Once in his office, and seated behind his desk, Geert politely asked, "Now, Mr. Andrews with the Internal Revenue Service, how might I be of assistance to you . . . and your government?"

So much for subtleties thought Andrews—switching to Phase Two. "Mr. Geert, we find irregularities from time to time that jump out at us and get our attention. In this case we have reason to believe that some group might be using Swiss banks to wire and hide funds. Funds that may have come from illegal or improper sources."

"Well, Mr. Andrews, we are a world bank," answered Geert.

The junior associate looked for traces of sarcasm. Perhaps he was just sizing him up or trying to intimidate his *youth*. Andrews played calm. "Of course."

"Have they broken U.S. laws or pose a terrorist threat?" asked Geert. "Those things appear to be you American's bigger concern these days."

"Not that we know."

"Have they laundered money?"

"We aren't certain."

"Are they U.S. citizens?" The banker delivered.

"We have reason to believe it does pertain to U.S. citizens," answered Andrews, but the fact that the Swiss banker had made it a point to ask *that* particular question, puzzled him. Did he know something? Was he trying (discretely) to aid the U.S. or was he merely offering up a red herring?

"You see Mr. Andrews, we boast having very private clientele and due to the secrecy expected, no demanded, by people of wealth, we can't just go giving names to everyone who asks." Smiling, he added, "We have clients from 163 countries in our system. Certainly, you understand."

"Mr. Geert. This *organization*, based on our estimates, has brought in almost $10 billion." His voice grew more demanding, adding, "$10 billion that we think taxes are owed on, owed to the U.S. government. I think other countries would be equally as concerned with such a large unpaid tax bill."

"This is the first inquiry we have—" the banker stopped, realizing he may have just admitted to some knowledge of *their* existence.

"So, you do know who I am seeking information about?" Andrews seized the moment.

"Actually, not at all," Geert insisted.

"One would think that after 2010, when we caught Swiss banks red-handed attempting to teach your clients how to evade taxes, that you might be a little more agreeable in an open dialog."

"Mr. Andrews, I made time today to see you." Geert stood offering his hand. "Perhaps, we should have spoken on the phone before you made your way here?"

"I'll be speaking with someone in your government later today," Andrews bluffed, wondering if the banker could be snookered by a young, low-level. IRS associate. "Maybe there is some need to inform all 163 of those countries about this $10 billion dollar organization, and possible tax law violations."

There was dead silence. It had become a game of chicken, each wanting to save face but not wanting to simply give in. Then, suddenly, they both smiled.

"Call me tomorrow. Here is my card," Geert said. "I'll see if I can be of more help with you then."

***

Will knocked on the door of a stately home. He knew it well, having grown up in Highland Park. An attractive woman in her late 40s answered the door to a surprised look.

"Mom."

"Will!" she hugged him warmly, Will was a little caught off guard not knowing his appearance would be so welcomed. He hugged back. "When did you get back? Why didn't you call?"

"Mom, I wasn't going to miss Christmas."

"Will, you don't know what you did to me. Every time I would hear of another killing in Mexico, I became paralyzed with fear."

"Mom, I was all right. We all were."

"Will, I have prayed every day since you've been gone."

"Mom, you saw me in October and I send emails almost daily."

"Yes, but seeing you here on this side of the border makes all the difference in the world," she said. "And now with those drug cartels taking people hostage and demanding money—"

"Hey, I'm here. I'm all right," Will said. "Where's Jimmy?"

"Your brother is with your sister and his new girlfriend and I don't want to talk about it."

"What's that supposed to mean?"

"I don't want to talk about it," she demanded.

"What is it? Is she not from the 214 area code?"

"Worse than that and I'm not saying anything more."

"Well, whatever. Sounds like typical Dallas pretension," he said dismissing his mother's comments. "What's the game plan for Christmas? Are we doing it here or at Grandma's?"

"We'll do Christmas Eve here tomorrow night and Christmas Day at your grandparents," she informed him. "Have you called your father?"

"No, I thought I'd see the look on his face when I got here."

"First, I need you to run to the mall and pick up a gift for your Father. It's paid for, I just can't leave now."

"Fine, I just hope I don't run into anyone I know."

***

"Honey, I'll be home for Christmas. I promise," Andrews said. "Trust me, the Swiss celebrate Christmas, too. How are you holding up?" He continued to assure his wife, nodding to himself while trying to catch SkyNews and CNN—he was never that good at multitasking. "Honey, I'll leave tomorrow. The latest flight is around 1 so I don't have much time, but I will make that flight.

"Uh huh . . . Mmm . . . any contractions? Hold off until I get home." Something moved by the door. "Honey, I gotta go."

He watched as an envelope slipped under the door, then looked at the doorknob for movement—nothing.

He grabbed the envelope, opened it and read "Meet tomorrow morning. 21 Rue Maltstrasse, 0800."

"OK," he thought, "but who was he to meet?"

He put on his pants, jerked the door opened, stepped out into the hall, and saw no one. The long hallway was empty.

He ran around the corner and right into an older couple. He apologized profusely and then retreated back to his room, where the phone was ringing.

"Honey, sorry about hanging up like that . . . honey?" Hearing no response, he called her name but silence only greeted him. Now suspicious, he hung up.

***

"Will! So long, no see!" His brother greeted him with a hug. "When did you get back in town?"

"Just this morning."

"Well, I guess your timing is good because we have gifts for you."

"Cricket! How's my favorite sister?" Will asked as she walked into the room. "How's life at SMU?"

"Boring, but it is my last year."

"Any sorority sisters that did not go home for the break that you could hook me up with?"

"I'm not 'hooking up' my brother," she insisted. "You're too old."

"I didn't say 'hook up with your brother,'" Will laughed. "Plus, since when was twenty-five considered old?"

"You're so gross."

Will laughed harder. He had always picked on Cricket. Now she was growing up, about to graduate, and he still treated her like he did when she was eight. Maybe it was time to grow up. On *The Island* he was the one in charge, the one who had to be grown up, but now he was home and it was Christmas—an excuse to cut loose, to relax.

Suddenly, something, no someone, caught his eye. "*Whoa!*" he thought to himself. She *did* have a sorority sister and she was holding out on her deserving brother.

"Cricket! You should be ashamed," Will scolded as he walked across the room. "Hi, I am Cricket's very single, good-looking oldest brother, and you are?"

"My name is Anna," the lovely object of Will's attention said. She was a hottie and had that thick Latin accent he so loved.

Seductively, Will took her hand and asked, "Are you in my sister's sorority?"

"No, Will," said Jimmy as he slid to her side "Umm, she's with me but, thanks for the endorsement."

"Wow. So, how cool of me to embarrass myself the first chance I get?" admitted Will, embracing the embarrassment. "First impressions, huh."

"I love it," laughed Cricket without any hint of discretion,

"Sounds like I missed something big," proclaimed Will's father as he entered the room.

"Dad," Will reached out to his father expecting a handshake. Instead, he got a hug. Will was taken aback. His father hadn't hugged him since, well he couldn't remember if he had ever hugged him.

"Son, you're looking good I haven't seen you since July? August? You know, you've had your Mom pretty worried being in Mexico with all those killings and kidnappings, but now you're home. Nice Christmas surprise."

Now he reached out and shook Will's hand, but something in the shake felt *odd* and out of place. He looked down at Will's hands, turned them upright and said, "Those aren't the hands of a working man, son. Do you just supervise down there?"

Will had no response. He wasn't sure if this was an attempt to belittle him, compliment him, or just to make small talk. Will thought about an insult to give right back at him, telling him that the closest thing he came to a working man was when he spoke with the lawn keeper at his home. "No," he thought. "just let it pass."

***

Once at the mall, Will checked his phone for news. He scanned the business section, as had become his daily routine. The headline "Mundo Lottery Billions" caught his eye. He grinned as he read the article. Noticing that it was by Reuters, bolstered his confidence to an even higher level. He looked around wishing to share the news with someone, but it was futile as there was no one he could trust.

Will thought of the power he now held. His cash could buy anyone in this mall and he knew it. He caught himself falling into the Dallas arrogance (chutzpa that couldn't possibly come back to hurt him) but, he choose to bask in it just a little longer, thinking "I am Will Hoke, future billionaire—"

"Will?"

He turned, and there she was, the most beautiful woman any man could ever desire. His heart blocked his throat. His mind was blank. He fought to gain his composure.

"Karina," he uttered trying to act nonchalant (even as his eyes betrayed him). "How are you?"

Not knowing what would be proper, Will stuck his hand out to shake, but Karina moved in with a hug. Will's arms gently encircled her body as they had so many times before. He wanted to squeeze her and feel her heartbeat. He wanted to smell her neck and run his fingers through her long black hair.

The moment felt so familiar it was as if they had only parted ways yesterday. Will tightened his embrace as if to make up for the five years since he last held her.

Karina loosened her embrace. Will drew back, attempting to cover his obvious act of adoration. "How is your family?" he blurted out.

"They are fine. My daughter turned three last month and Mark and I are back here in Dallas with his job."

"And how are your parents?" Will asked, making sure there was no doubt which family he was asking about.

"Oh, they are fine. Dad is talking about retiring and my brother is getting his act together. He's going to community college in the Valley."

"Good for him," Will offered, in an effort to appear concerned, when, truth be told, he was only interested in her. Ever since their relationship had ended Will had used other women in a vain attempt to replace her or dull the pain. He knew she was married and that alone ended any hopes he had of ever being with her again. He realized it was fruitless, but she still had his heart.

"What are you doing now?"

"Karina, you wouldn't believe me if I told you—"

At that moment, a sales consultant interrupted Will and informed him that his package was ready. She placed it on the counter and handed Will the receipt. As she walked away Will turned his focus back on Karina.

"I saw Robert a month ago. He said you were doing well."

"Really? He failed to mention seeing you."

"It was at the airport in Corpus. We were boarding separate planes."

Thinking that was a sign, Will thought he should open up to Karina about how he had failed her, failed himself, when he allowed himself to be dictated to by his father. Did she know the depth of his betrayal? Had she forgiven him? Did she even care?

"Karina," Will said with a contrite tone, "I just want you to know—"

"There you are," said a male intruder. Will turned and made eye contact with him as Karina reached out to hoist the young girl he carried. She nestled the youngster on her hip and turned back to Will.

"Mark, this is Will," Karina explained.

"The Will?" Mark asked, knowing full well it was Karina's old flame. He looked to see if there was any spark left between the two. While still gauging the situation, Mark reached out to shake Will's hand.

"Yes," Karina answered, refusing to give into any tension. "Do either of you recognize the other from SMU?"

They both said no (not that they would have admitted it anyway), Mark continued to size up Will. Feeling out of place, Will quickly sought to diffuse the awkward moment.

"And who is this here?" Will asked pointing to the young girl.

"This is Katie, our endless bundle of energy," said Karina.

Will leaned down and offered, "Katie, I bet you just turned three years old a month ago."

The little girl turned away.

Will shrugged and said, "I guess I just have that affect on women."

"So, you've been seeing Mary for some time now?" queried Karina.

Will looked startled and confused. How did she know about Mary? Was *this* a sign?

"Nope, back in September I got a text. Welcome to Dumpville. Population me."

"I'm sorry—didn't know—wouldn't have brought it up."

Mark didn't seem comfortable hearing this chatter between Will and Karina. This was, after all, any man's biggest fear: having his wife run into an ex-lover. On the other hand, Will was dying inside. He knew what he was missing and what Mark wasn't. Almost five years had passed yet it was as fresh, and painful, as if it had happened five minutes ago.

"Look, I have a house full of people and I need to get back, it was great running into you." With that Will turned and headed straight to the door. His steps quickened as he neared the exit. Although he knew better, he turned his to steal one last glimpse of his life's love. Maybe she was looking back, too.

He glanced back and did indeed see a pair of eyes following his exit but those eyes belonged to Mark. Will departed, now knowing it was he who flinched. No longer was he on top of the world.

The sales consultant walked back to the counter and noticed the package still resting there. She looked around not seeing Will or anyone else. She turned to another sales lady and informed her that Will had left his purchase.

Power

The next morning Andrews walked the streets of Zurich searching for 21 Rue Maltstrasse. Reaching his destination he found Matthias Geert, perhaps Mr. Geert would not be so rigid today.

"Good morning, Mr. Andrews," Geert offered. "There is a nice park in which to speak." He motioned in the direction of the park. As they walked, Geert pulled out a pack of cigarettes and offered one to Andrews. Andrews declined, in fact, he hated cigarettes. As they continued to walk, Andrews noticed that they were no longer alone. Two much bigger, serious looking types were shadowing them. Andrews stopped.

"Do not be alarmed," said Geert. "They are with me and only here for *our* protection."

"What exactly do we need to be protected from?" inquired Andrews.

"Oh, nothing really. You must understand that in my position, I must operate with caution, even here in peaceful little Switzerland," he joked in an effort to lighten the mood. "They are security for the bank."

"You wouldn't be attempting to intimidate a trusted associate with the IRS, would you now Mr. Geert?"

"No, I merely wanted to get an early start this morning because I have a full day."

"Well, how did you know where I was staying?"

"Mr. Andrews, you are paranoid. All IRS people stay there when visiting. I assumed you did not make your own accommodations and would be staying there as well."

"True, but look, all I want to know is if there are Americans using your bank, If they are U.S. citizens, then they must be filing quarterly. Every three months, that is U.S. law."

"But, your filing year has not even been completed. Aren't you jumping the gun, Mr. Andrews or has the IRS become preemptive in its efforts to collect taxes based on assumptions?" the Swiss banker held. "Sounds like a U.S. problem."

"Mr. Geert, this is obviously is a concern to my superiors and they have ordered me here to seek your cooperation. Am I getting it or not?"

"Mr. Andrews, as I said yesterday, I am bound to uphold certain privacies of our clients. You said yourself that nothing illegal had been done," Geert reasoned. "Call me when, no if, they break any laws. I wish you a safe trip back to the States, oh, and Merry Christmas."

And like that, Geert's car pulled up, the security duo opened the door, and he was gone. It was as if the whole meeting had been choreographed. Andrews felt foolish, even a bit stupid. He had been schooled just like a rube. He wondered if his Alabaman accent had surfaced. He couldn't help but think he was still being watched as he stood there. He reached down and pulled out his phone. He began to talk, as if in conversation with someone on the other end, "Sir. I think they fell for it."

***

Christmas Day at the Hoke Mansion was filled with the typical settings from years past. Poppy Hoke had been the mayor of Dallas in the early '80s and had a hand in bringing the Dallas Mavericks to Texas. An oil man all his life, he went bust with all the other independents in the mid- to late-'80s when the world oil glut sank Texas crude so low that it wasn't worth digging for. Before that, he had been linked to the Hunt brothers attempt to corner the silver market—because they shared a horse named Silver Saddle. That was all the *evidence* the feds needed to charge him as an accessory. Charges were later dropped, but only after millions went to attorneys. To this day, silver was not allowed in his home.

Having finished eating, the clan moved to the massive living room where a 20 foot tree adorned the room. The material goods were obvious with the number of gifts beneath the tree.

The gifts are of discriminating taste, and all tags are left on so that the women might return them to Neiman Marcus, Dolce & Gabbana, Ralph Lauren, etc. and get what they really wanted. The men got new designer golf clubs, Super Bowl tickets, bourbon and Cuban cigars. How the women scored illegal Cubans remained a mystery to Will.

He looked across the room at Anna, she was beautiful. She reminded him of Karina, and remembered how ill at ease Karina had been at Christmas five years ago. She couldn't compete with his family's money. Only now did Will feel guilty for insisting she stay in Dallas that Christmas. Oh, how low she must have felt, and that the one who loved her so much had put her through so much. He had been so self-centered and selfish. He felt a shame come over him and he recalled.

Glancing back at Anna, Will wondered if maybe Jimmy should have the same concern for her. But then again Anna, seemed was quite calm and at ease. She was able to lose the heavy Latin accent when she wanted and then use it when needed.

For a moment, Will longed for love as he once had known it, but for now, it was being set aside for love of his millions, his multi-millions—.

"Will!" Cricket screamed. "Thanks, so much!"

Startled out of his daydream, Will nodded.

"Well, what did you get, Cricket?" Poppy Hoke asked.

"Roundtrip tickets to Europe, for four! All first class!"

"Will, does Cricket know something she's blackmailing you with?" smirked Poppy.

True, Will had never been so lavish in Christmases past and the thought that such nice gifts might cause suspicion, never occurred to him. He attempted to cover himself, "Trust me, I got them cheap on an internet special and, by the way, that's also your graduation gift for May."

Cricket was still giddy, "Well, they couldn't have been that cheap, they are open-ended tickets. Aww thanks, Will."

"Well, look. Those are for you and three girls. No guys. I'm not having my sister skank around Europe on my nickel." Sometimes it felt good being the older brother, he thought.

"Gee Will, now you're taking some of the luster off," Cricket said.

"Will, you shouldn't have," said his Mom. "Four roundtrip tickets to the Holy Land! Look Hon, we've never been."

"Hell, what did you in Mexico Will, rob a bank?" his uncle Tom joked.

Will lowered his head while venting his eyes towards his father. There it was that suspicious, jaundiced look of disapproval. He couldn't even escape his father's disapproval on Christmas

Day, no less. Will looked away, then, slowly came back to his father, who was still staring.

"Hey Will," called out his brother. "Where's my gift? You actually like me, so mine's got to be better than Cricket's."

"Anna, I am sorry that this family is so rude to be doing all of this in front of you but, Jimmy insisted—".

"Umm, Mom, your timing is pretty spot on, here," Jimmy meekly broke in. He glanced over at Anna as if to say, "this is it." She nodded. He delayed, looked at Will and his father, then finally said, "Last week, I asked Anna to marry me and she said 'YES' . . ."

Jimmy turned to Anna and assured her it was OK and she lifted her left hand revealing an engagement ring and a rather nice one at that. The room fell silence for a brief second. Then erupted in celebration, with Cricket the most joyous of all. The new, future mother-in-law appeared less than thrilled. It was all too quick for her. She glanced over at Will.

Will tilted his eyes toward his father. He thought now he would no longer be son Number Two. Ha! But instead of the disapproval his father had expressed over Karina, he seemed genuinely pleased. "Unbelievable," Will thought. "Dad's an actor but is this for real? Unfrickingbelievable." Rage shot through Will's heart.

Will stood up and gave Jimmy and Anna a hug. "Awesome Anna. Welcome to the family." Will slipped out of the living room down the hall to a game room, turned on the TV, and sat down. Only to stand back up, grab his keys, and slip out.

***

Back at the rig, the workers watched the jackpots adding up and continued contacting winners. The workers had expected that with the Christmas season upon them, people would back off buying lottery tickets. Robert had expected a slow down as well, until he come up with a great idea. He added a feature where people could give lottery tickets as Christmas gifts! While explaining to the workers that they would be working through Christmas Robert unveiled the feature, Explaining that anyone could pre-pay any amount to give as a *gift card*. However generous the giver was wanting to be, $10, $20, $100, or more. They could simply email the *gift card*, and the recipient could use it to play.

Robert was sure the *gift cards* would result in a spike in business so, to calm the employees, they were each given a $5,000 Christmas bonus. No one seemed to mind. Attitudes adjusted.

In fact, the small group of eight took some of their bonus and wagered as to when the 20,000 winner would be picked. It was almost assured that it would be before January 1st and a wager seemed like a good way to alleviate some of the boredom that came with living on the rig.

Each employee put $1,000 of their "new wealth" into a winner-take-all pot. After all, it was tax free and they would still have $4,000 of their unexpected bonus no matter what.

***

Hitting the nightlife in Dallas, Will moved through the crowd alone. He held his drink high in an attempt not to spill. It was hard for him because he had had a few and his vision and walk were both *blurred*. Surprisingly, his speech wasn't. It was just enough alcohol that his charm was higher than usual, but not enough to dull his realization that business on the rig had come at a rather steep price. The lack of a woman in his life.

He hadn't had any affection of note since Mary. It made little sense to her that he was off in some far away land bringing amenities to the poor. At first, it had been admirable but over time she saw her friends with their steady (and there in person) boyfriends and how they were making their mark in life and soon she began to view Will much like his father did. She wanted security and a future. Having a slacker for a boyfriend wasn't what she had bargained for. So, in September, she ended it.

Will looked around the room. Suddenly, he felt old. Unlike in the past when he knew most of the faces if not the names, he found himself in the midst of strangers. And even worse they all seemed much younger than him. Even in his drunken state, he felt as if he did not belong. "Still," he thought, "gotta love Dallas women—"

"Will?" He turned to a female voice calling out. "Will Hoke?" He heard the voice again. He turned the other way and saw a vaguely familiar face. A very attractive familiar face. "Will, it's me, Holly. I was a Pi Phi with Mary," she explained.

"Yeah. You were a couple of years behind her, right?" Will reasoned. He did remember her and always felt guilty for stealing looks at her at the sorority functions. She was young and at the time he and Mary were doing all right.

"Actually, three," she corrected. "She was such a bitch to me."

"You should read the last email she sent me," Will laughed. "It was a Dear Will letter."

"You're not seeing each other anymore?"

"No, I guess she got a sudden case of better taste."

"Then come to my table," she demanded and Will was willing.

Once at the table he recognized some faces and felt more at ease. He did, however, want to get out of this bar and be alone with Holly. A round of shots were brought and Will was *forced* to join the group. He didn't want to, but it was a small price to pay to be with this beautiful young blonde that came in a very small package.

"Will, did you have a good Christmas?" Holly asked. "What are you doing now?"

"OK, I guess," he answered followed by, "I work on an oil rig."

"You lie," she laughed. "Seriously, what do you do?"

"I own my own business . . . I print money," he said in a cocky way.

"If you're not going to be serious," she said in an irritated manner. "Will, I'm already getting bored."

Wow, he thought. She is a typical Dallas Daddy's girl diva. Sensing she was playing him, Will turned the tables.

"You know, you are so attractive, I can't help but think what great looking children we would have."

"William Hoke. You are bad," she said as if she had never been propositioned before. "Bad," she repeated now as if she was bad herself.

"Now I'm bored," said Will. "Let's get outta here."

***

Agent Andrews entered his office. It was the day after Christmas. He didn't understand why he was expected to be working, especially when there were bowl games on. His attitude was not one of Christmas joy. His secretary was not so joyful either.

"He wants you to see him first thing," Andrew's secretary told him.

"What's his mood?"

"Usual. No Merry Christmas or 'how's the family, Julie?'," she remarked.

Andrews walked down the hall and entered his boss' office. "Morning, sir."

Getting straight to the point, the senior manager asked, "What did you find out in Zurich? I don't have a report yet."

"Well, of course," thought Andrews. "What did you expect? I got home at 8 p.m. on Christmas Eve, then had Christmas with the family. I have a family, you know. A pregnant wife, due any day. How was your Christmas alone with your cat?"

Then, he opted to be more political and said, "Well sir, I got home on Christmas Eve just in time for Christmas Day with family, and now here I am first thing, the day after Christmas."

"Yes, well I'd appreciate something soon," he said. "What did you find out? Are there Americans running this lottery thing?"

"No sir. I didn't find any names or nationalities."

"And what was the bank's attitude? Since we now have treaties making it so their banks can no longer be tax shelters for hiding money."

"He appeared very confident in denying my requests," said Andrews.

"Or, maybe he didn't feel so threatened by me sending such a young associate."

"I doubt that, sir," Andrews insisted. "I represent the authority of the U.S. and we are the greatest ally the Swiss have."

"Yes," agreed the senior. "They must be running tens of billions thru those banks to be so willing to buck us on this."

"Are we done here?"

"No. I want you to take a trip south. You need to call the desk and make arrangements for the Caymans."

"Caymans? We don't even have a treaty with them. They would never talk."

"I've never seen someone protest a free trip to the Caribbean."

"Sir, my wife is due any day now with our first—"

"Oh, the first kid is always late. You'll be back in time. Besides the sooner you leave, the quicker you'll be back."

***

Will woke up in unfamiliar surroundings. Clearing his head, he looked down to his left and there she was. Still attractive. He was relieved that beer goggles had not clouded his vision. He smiled. He thought about what she had said about his Mary. "Was this just her way to get back at her sorority sister? Was it his way of getting back at Mary? Either way, what's done, is done," he thought. "Closure."

Waking up, Holly asked, "You still here?"

Now he really didn't feel guilty about the one nighter.

Will turned to see if he was being *told* to leave. He didn't want conflict. He had left Christmas at the Hoke house to avoid it, now this. "Please, I'll just leave."

"Are you serious?" Holly asked. "I'm was just messing with you. You were a lot more charming last night."

"Oh, really? How so?"

"Well, you ended up here."

"Only because you kept feeding me shots."

"Will, you were already pretty lit last night when we met."

"Oh, yeah. Well I just had a lot of things on my mind, that I wanted to get off my mind," Will admitted.

"Like going to work on an oil rig?"

"What?!" Will snapped.

"You told me last night that you work on an oil rig."

"Yeah, well I'll explain it later," Will said. "Say, what are you doing tomorrow?"

"Nothing. School's out until the 15th."

"School?"

"Yes, we don't start back for three more weeks."

"Holly, how old are you?"

"Will, I graduate in May. I'm 22 . . . you like 'em younger?"

"Right now, I just like them."

"Why did you ask about tomorrow?" Holly asked.

"Care to fly to LA for a few days?" Will asked.

"I have a date on Friday."

"Break it."

***

Back at his parent's home, Will let himself in the back door only to be greeted by the family having a late breakfast.

"Someone's wearing the same clothes from last night," Will's father observed.

Kissing his mother, she noted that he smelled of cigarettes and alcohol.

"Brother, where did you go last night?" asked Jimmy.

"I was lead to believe that Jimmy was the lady's man," said Anna. Her comment got the biggest laugh.

"Nah, I just didn't want to drive home last night," Will said.

"I can certainly smell why," his mother repeated.

"Yes, Mom," Will answered sarcastically. "I got wasted last night, OK?"

"What did you leave for?" Jimmy asked. "One minute you're here, then gone."

"Never mind," Will insisted. "Don't interrogate me in front of my future sister-in-law." He smiled her way, then asked. "So Anna, what's your story?"

"Will!" several voices reprimanded him for his apparent rudeness.

"No. I meant no disrespect. I mean like I'm behind the curve here," he explained. "So bring me up to date. How did you meet my brother? Where did you go to school? Where are you from? You know, the down low."

"No problem. I was born in Mexico City. My father is a banker, my mother was a teacher but retired now and I am in a Masters program here at SMU."

"Where did you do your undergrad?"

"At Brown."

"Must be some bank," Will said, shooting a *now I get it* look at his father. "Next question—"

"Will, that's enough," his mother interrupted.

Ignoring his mother, Will asked. "You got a sister?"

"Will, how vulgar," insisted his mother.

"Mom, I'm trying to be complimentary here."

"Oh, why thank you," Anna said, looking at Jimmy for his approval. "My turn."

"Turn for what?" asked Will.

"My turn for questions."

"Didn't my brother speak glowingly about me already?" Will asked.

"Of course, but recently where have you been? Jimmy said something about you being in the *Norte*?"

"Norte?"

"Oh, we call it *El Norte* back home in Mexico," Anna said. "Aren't you concerned about your safety with all the cartel murders and the kidnappings? You know they ransom *gringos*," she joked.

"We keep our heads down."

"In what part of *El Norte* are you doing this great wonderful thing?"

"In a little town about an hour from Monclova, just south of Monterrey,"

"Monclova is north of Monterrey," Anna corrected him.

"Yeah, I know," Will said. "Just checking *your* geography." Changing the subject, he asked Jimmy, "What are your plans for tomorrow around noon?"

"I'm driving Anna over to the Fort Worth Stockyards. Anna has never been so we're doing the touristy thing. Why?"

"I have a trip we can all go on. It will be three days," Will whispered. "Come. I'll have you back well before New Years Eve. Promise."

***

"I can't believe they let you come here with me. You've only been with the bureau for six months. . . . Unbelievable," said Andrews.

"Hey, I didn't ask to come. I'm missing the Michigan game tonight unless we find some way to watch it here," said a young, single, man.

"Hey, it's not a major bowl game," said Andrews. "Face it. It's the *Suck Bowl.*"

"At least we are in a bowl game this year".

"Well, I'm just surprised that our boss liked anyone, much less you," said Andrews. "Spivey, you are everything I would think he would dislike. You're young, single and loud."

"Yeah, I sure never saw myself working for the IRS—".

"I still don't," Andrews agreed. "And I don't understand why they sent us here, we don't have financial agreements with the Caymans."

"The Director said to mingle in the high-end bars," reminded Spivey.

"Oh yeah, that's going to work well for me," said Andrews in a sarcastic tone. "Women can smell a married man with a pregnant wife at home. I'm a real catch."

"Well, I was here for Spring Break," said Spivey. "Lots of Dutch chicks that year. Scored!" He laughed at his own joke.

While checking in they both noted how nice it was that the IRS had sprung for rooms at the Ritz-Carlton.

***

Will had to add a couple of rooms at check in. Their number had now grown from four to ten, mostly last minute girlfriends.

"Will, how did you spring for this?" asked Jimmy. "You've got three rooms and a suite?"

"No. I combined three other suites with the presidential suite," said Will.

"What is wrong with you? How can you afford this?"

"Jimmy, I won the lottery."

"Will, don't be stupid. No one we know even plays the lottery."

"Ahh, don't be so sure Jimbo," Will mocked him for his naïveté. "What people do in the dark or behind closed doors, remains unknown."

"Something is fishy," observed Jimmy.

"Fishy? How long have you been dating Miss Mexico there?"

"What's it to you?" demanded Jimmy. "Are you pissed because she looks like Karina?"

"She looks nothing like Karina," Will snapped, holding his hands out in a defensive fashion as if to deflect the issue. "Look, we're here for three nights of wasted fun in LA. I didn't fly you here to fight nor to explain myself."

"Will, is the game tonight?" asked Stu.

"Tomorrow night."

"Game?" asked Jimmy.

"Oh, I got six tickets to the Mavs-Lakers game."

"Unreal," sighed Jimmy.

Suddenly, Will's phone rang. He said little, mostly listened. Then he grinned and said, "Thanks for calling. Remember call, don't text." Then Will hung up.

For those close enough to hear, he assured them that all is OK. "Nothing," Will shrugged to no one in particular then gathered Robert, Charles and Stu and then motioned them to come close. He leaned in and whispered, "Guys, *The Island* just called. We are seven away from 20,000." He gave them the thumbs up.

"Gentlemen, we are all worth at least $700 million each!"

***

The Cayman people are known for being hospitable. The banks . . . not so much. Now, for the client, they are quite accommodating, but for the outsider asking questions, they are a closed door. Andrews and Spivey hit every bank they could, but the result was the same. No dice.

Andrews felt as if he was just going thru the motions since his focus was 1,500 miles away and ready to deliver. Spivey, on the other hand, was happy to be there and ready to party.

"Hey, tomorrow might be better," said Spivey. It almost sounded encouraging, but Andrews wasn't buying it. "Have another beer. These Caybrews aren't bad."

"Yeah, but at $8 a pop, I'm taking it easy," said Andrews.

Making eyes at young international women, Spivey turned to the bartender with an approving look. The bartender asked, "Do you like what you see?"

"Of course," said Spivey. "Is she local?"

"You never know," said the bartender. "The world comes to Cayman for the sun, the beach, the nightlife. We get a lot of Brits, but maybe she's Dutch."

"A woman like that would only want a high roller," said Spivey. "Or, at least someone who just won the lottery."

"Lottery?" laughed the bartender. "Then, you should talk to him." He pointed to a young black man entertaining a small crowd of attractive women. "He won the lottery. I know him long time. We used to work together just three months ago, then BANG! He win the lottery."

"The Caymans have a lottery?" asked Andrews, suddenly interested in the conversation.

"No, he won with a ticket that was given to him when we were waiters at another hotel," the bartender said. "I got a ticket, too. But I don't win."

"What's his name?" asked Spivey.

"Trevor," said the bartender. "He's a good guy. Go talk to him, the lucky bastard."

***

The Los Angeles streets are filled with beautiful people. Many have just stepped off the bus that very day, no friends, no home, with only a dream to become someone in entertainment. Everyone has a story and Will and the group had been partying this night trying to add to their own stories. They were full of hugs and laughter.

Spotting a club, known for great nightlife and celebrity, they got in line to enter. Stu walked up to the bouncer at the door, bypassing those standing in the front of the line. He approached a huge black man who appeared to be in charge. "Who do I need to see to get in?" Stu asked.

"Do I know you?" the bouncer demanded.

"No, man. We are in from out of state and looking to party."

"Well look, Small Time, I got my regulars, I got my celebs, I got my women who will do me just to get in, then three notches down, I got you."

"Whoaaaa!" interrupts Robert. "Everyone knows this place and we are in town for the Mavs game, just looking for some fun."

"Then, we got Disneyland," said the bouncer.

"Look . . . we got off on the wrong foot here," offered Robert, who stuck his hand out to shake and slipped the bouncer a couple of hundreds in hopes that will open the velvet rope.

Looking at the hundreds, the bouncer announced that he would check and see what he could.

"What did you give him?" Will whispered.

"A couple of hundreds," said Robert.

"I think he's playing us," said Charles.

"Hold on," said Will. "Let's walk next door here and give him ten minutes." Turning to the big man, Will pointed and said, "Don't dupe us, big man."

They sat down by the window, ordered a round, and watched. Will sat and brooded. With his new independence and wealth he should be in control. Problem was, only he knew he was wealthy. His anger at being so easily dismissed really got to him. "Don't they know who I am?" he wondered.

Actually, they didn't.

Will stood and walked out of the bar. He dismissed the voices inquiring where he was going.

Approaching the bouncer, Will was told to stop. "I told you I'd see what I can do."

"The name of the owner," demanded Will.

"Do what, little man?" the bouncer shot back.

"My friend gave you $200. I'll make it an even $1,000 if you simply bring the owner out," said Will.

"You got a thousand on you?" asked the bouncer.

"Only one way you're going to find out," said Will.

Slowly, the bouncer radioed inside with Will's request.

The group watched through the window while Will stood alone in the dark LA night. They openly wondered what was going on, debated if they should stay or go help him, if he even needed help.

"This had better be good," a man in his late-thirties announced as he walked out of the club, turning toward the bouncer, he added. "Tyrone here has never called me out before because he knows it is a *fireable* offense."

"Well, Tyrone," Will asked once more. "Are you letting me and my friends in here?"

"Not yet," he said.

Turning to the owner, Will said. "Sir, my name is William Hoke, I am from Dallas. I want to buy your club."

Turning to Tyrone, and with a smug look on his face, the thirty something owner said, "You got me out for this? You are fired." Then he turned to Will and said, "Go back to Texas, you can't afford this place."

"We are not done here," Will demanded.

"How much do think a place like this goes for?"

"You tell me."

"OK, Mister William Hoke from Dallas," the owner said. "Two point five mil. Cash."

"Done," said Will. "You got papers?" Turning back to the bouncer, Will added, "By the way, Tyrone. You're not fired."

"Just like that?" asked the owner.

"If you can put something down in writing. Now," said a firm Will.

"Follow me."

As Will followed the owner, he noticed the love and attention he got from those still standing in line hoping to gain entrance. He saw the respect the bouncers gave him. Although slightly buzzed from his early night, Will tried to sum up the owner. Looking at his ponytail, it was so typical of well, a thirty-year old cheesy club owner. Should he drop the deal altogether? Will was conflicted.

"Your timing could not have been better. In fact, it is perfect. If I didn't know better I would be sure someone had told, but no one knows," said the owner in his arrogant way. "After the new year, I was going to put the club up for sale."

Once inside, Will read the contract and noticed something that did not seem quite right. "Are you the sole owner. No corporation?"

"That's what you see," said the owner.

"You own the building?"

"Yes, I do."

"No wives or ex-wives to be, no silent partners?"

"None at all."

The club owner handed another paper to Will.

"Just a one-page contract?" Will asked.

"Short and simple."

Will read the contract and asked if there was a copy.

Writing his name on the dotted line, Will announced, "Done and done," he smiled a buzzed grin and said, "I'll pay now."

"I'll send you wiring instructions," said the club owner.

"No need. I'll use my card now," said Will.

"But, I said cash."

"Will a debit card do?"

"Do you have that much in a checking account?"

"I do and you'll see the funds immediately."

The club owner is impressed but stops. "You know I'll have to pay 2 to 3% of that in charges. That's over $75 thousand dollars in lost fees—"

"And, you'd be paying a broker 6% to someone else if I don't buy this now and that's over 150 thousand you lose!" Will pointed out. "Don't play games with me."

At that time, three more bouncers walked in and stood behind Will. He looked, but the alcohol inside him refused to give in.

Will continued and said, "Say, I put $50,000 down now on my card, that's only a $1,000 loss to you, the rest I wire you OR you come to the Cayman Islands and I'll pay the rest in an account no one can trace. No taxes for you."

It was an irresistible offer and he accepted. Will stood up, took his copy, swiped his card for $50,000 and said he appreciated the deal.

The $50,000 cleared.

The club owner laughed and said, as he looked to his bouncers, "You are a very trusting man, Mr. Will Hoke."

"Not really," said Will. "I paid the $50,000 now. I suggest you re-work the papers to reflect that and call me tomorrow. We'll void this contract and I'll sign that one when it is ready. I'm here for 36 more hours, then, my plane leaves. My private plane."

"And if I don't write up a new contract, then your money is mine," laughed the owner. He looked up at the bouncers who laughed, too. "I could deny we ever had a deal. I am certain these fellows would back me up."

"Yes, but you won't do that," said Will.

"What makes you so sure and who are you to speak to me this way?" asked the owner.

"I know you won't deal in bad faith."

"And you don't think I can claim we never had an agreement as these guys take your contract from you?"

"No, because you love your life too much."

"You threatening me?"

"Do you love your life?" Will asked followed by, "Do any of you speak Spanish?"

The club owner looked around the room and got no response. He had no response either. "No, I don't. Why do you ask?"

Will, too looked around the room at the bouncers and the club owner. He leaned in and softly yet, sternly said, "Then it will be very hard for you to beg for your life with the people that I will have show up to your front door if this deal does not go through."

A look of fear came across the owner's face. No one would ever make a threat like that unless they were capable of doing it. His tactics of intimidation had failed. "You seemed like such a nice guy," said the owner.

"Yes I am, but I am just as mean as I am nice," said Will slowly adding, "And I am a very nice guy."

"Who are you?"

"What's the point," Will said and added a bluff. "I know all about you and your need to keep this secret. When can my plane pick you up?"

***

Exiting the club Will placed an additional $800 in Tyrone's massive hand. "Now walk across the street and get the rest of my party and personally escort them in. I am your new boss."

Learning

"So, you were given a $500 card that you could only use on the website MundoLottery.com, back in August or September?" asked agent Andrews. "And you played, and you won a million dollars. Do I have that straight?"

"Yes," answered Trevor.

"How long before you received your money?" asked Spivey.

"It was only a matter of days," said Trevor.

"How often did you play this game?" Spivey asked.

"Only once. I was a waiter for a press conference at the Ritz. Everyone got a $500 Visa card that was only good to play online. I got a card, the press got a card, *everyone* got one. They must have given out 200 at least. As far as I know, I was the only winner. Changed my life."

"How much total did you receive?" asked Andrews.

"I got $920 thousand. Cash," said Trevor. "So, while technically, I was not a millionaire, my club has made me one. I cleared $40 grand this month."

"Well, that's nice for you," said Andrews. "What can you tell us about the people you spoke with when you won the lottery?"

"Man, I'm telling you these guys don't do any wrong. They help people like me become rich."

"I understand you wanting to protect them, but they are in violation of U.S. tax laws along with laws in many other countries," explained Spivey.

"But, I only win the money and have no obligation to you to report anything. I am finished talking." As Trevor stood up to leave he added, "You have no jurisdiction over me and I wish only the best for them."

And with that, Trevor was gone. The agents looked at each other.

"Nothing," said Andrews. "We got nothing."

***

Waking up in suites overlooking West Hollywood, the hung over group began to emerge. Charles made his way to the dining table where the others had gathered. Wiping the cobwebs from his eyes, he asked if this was breakfast or lunch.

"Whatever you make it," answered Stu.

"If I never see another beer," said Charles, pausing for effect, ". . . it will be a shame." Then he broke into laughter at his own joke. No one joined in, probably because they were still hung over and really didn't want to see one so soon.

Breaking the stag conversation, a young female spoke up and asked an obviously overlooked question, "So did Will just walk up and buy the club last night? I didn't get what happened."

With Will absent from the table, none of the remaining three wanted to venture a guess. Everyone had been drinking, but Will had begun to exert more influence in more situations as of recent and this might have been a major blow to their privacy issues. Stu leaned into Robert and mumbled a question. "Did Will buy it or did we all buy it?"

Anna spoke up and offered an answer for all the behavior. "Oh, I'm sure he just greased the doorman or that manager," She offered.

"Greased?!" asked a shocked Jimmy. "How does an honest banker's daughter know a term like that?"

"What?" Anna asked.

"What are they teaching you at SMU law school?" laughed Jimmy. "Who is your professor? A teamster?"

"Stop it," laughed Anna. "It's a well-known term."

"Well, whatever he did, it worked," Robert offered while glancing back at his cohorts for support.

All the while, brother Jimmy sat back with a suspicious look and grumbled, "Yes, it did."

As if on cue, a spry, sober Will entered the room with a cell phone firmly attached to his ear. Speaking aloud and pointing for juice he could be overheard asking about tickets. The group listened but only heard one side of the conversation.

"There he is," announced Stu, turning his voice to feign a farmer's voice (more like what he though a farmer's voice would sound like), he delivered a "Mornin', Will."

Will acknowledged the group but continued his conversation, "No, I'll do twelve-five. I'm not doing fifteen." He motions again for juice and said, "That's for six tickets? Then, done. Fifteen. Now, question. Will you send a courier here to accept cash? Yes, fifteen in cash. You'll do it yourself? Then, let's do this as quick as you can. I'll be here. Call this cell and I'll meet you in the lobby. *Hasta*."

Will hung up, downed his juice, then turned to the group and announced, "We are *all* going to the game. Limo will be here at 6:30. Go shop, layout or whatever but we leave at 7:00, no later."

The girls screeched with happiness. The guys were already under the impression they were going so this was nothing new. Then Will stopped and cautioned, "Whoa, now we are not all sitting together, but most are good seats. We are not all court-side, I did what I could."

Brother Jimmy again looked at his brother with a judgmental eye.

***

The agents had found the Caymans less than helpful. All they got from the banks was rejection after rejection They were packed and on their way back to the U.S. As they strolled through the hotel lobby they recapped their misadventures.

"I expected this," said Andrews. "Even though they are a British territory, we have no treaty with the Caymans. No treaty, so they can give us the middle finger all day."

"Why would they even send us here then?" asked Spivey.

"Because, with the new administration, they have to show they are 'tough on tax evaders' and, our boss has his own political aspirations," said Andrews.

"So, we are just being used?"

"No, you got a trip to the Grand Caymans out of this, and our boss gets to look good to his superiors."

"Then, I wish they'd use me more," said Spivey.

"Well, since my wife is home about to deliver our first child, I can't get off this island fast enough."

They packed their luggage into the shuttle van and headed off toward the airport. They had not been on the island that long but a few of the sites they passed along the way already looked familiar. As they passed the part of town where they had talked with the lottery winner the previous night, Andrews spotted Trevor's bar.

"Stop the van!" Andrews ordered. He jumped out and ran to the bar. Once inside, he asked for Trevor. Told that it was only 7:30 and satisfied that Trevor was not around, he turned to leave, then there in front of him stood Trevor. "Surprise," said Andrews.

"Look, we spoke yesterday and I have nothing to say to you. I owe you nothing."

"Yes, you're right," said Andrews. "I just wanted to thank you for speaking with us. It took a lot of courage."

"Courage?" asked Trevor. "You can do nothing to me. It was nothing to talk with you."

"Yeah, I guess you are right," said Andrews in full compliance. "By the way, where did they take you for your shopping getaway, if you don't mind telling me?"

"I never was taken anywhere."

"Oh then, I guess maybe that's for other people. Not island workers. Sorry 'bout that."

"Wait! What do you mean?" demanded Trevor.

"It was my understanding that all winners were flown somewhere exotic for a shopping spree," explained Andrews. "I mean, they made a lot of money off you, so flying you to Paris or Milan or even Dubai would be nothing, even if you had to use your own winnings to buy things. Just saying. Sorry. Maybe they didn't think you would know better."

Angered by the thought that quite possibility he was considered a lowly waiter and didn't deserve a luxury trip to Paris, like the other winners, made Trevor feel a little betrayed. Never mind that because of Mundo Lottery he had more money now than he ever dreamt was possible, never mind that it was Mundo

Lottery who gave him the Visa card that allowed him to purchase a winning ticket.

And just like that, his loyalty changed.

"Know better?" Trevor angrily disputed. "I did live in Miami in my youth. I can tell you now that those boys are from the United States. I would start in Texas."

Andrews walked back to the van, smirking that a street-smart guy in the Caymans folded like a dime store umbrella in a gale force wind. Jumping back into the van, Spivey asked what just happened.

"Base hit," Andrews said. "Just a base hit."

***

Back in LA, the party of ten spent like there was no tomorrow. Money flowed and the guys—mainly Will—were king. Tired of watching and not knowing, Jimmy approached Will and said, "We need to talk."

Sensing his brother's potential admonition, Will deflected first with his own question. "What is up with you and Anna? Why so quick to marry? Is she pregnant? Are you not having a great time here?"

"Will, I don't need to talk about me," Jimmy answered. "I want to know where you are getting this money."

"What do you mean?"

"Let's not do this. I know what you have and this is unreal money you are spending. Christmas, these rooms, the plane out here, tickets to the game and what the hell did you tip those guys last night to get us in that club?!" Jimmy demanded. "Seriously, you're spending money like a cheesy drug lord of some sort!"

"A drug lord?" Will asked, slightly taken aback. "Cheesy. Dealing in cash only. Not so."

"Will, what are you trying to prove?"

"Nothing. I have nothing to prove."

"Then, what is up with all the show of money. You go away to Mexico, we have no idea where you are and—" suddenly, it all made sense. "How could everyone have been so dumb?" Jimmy thought.

"Will, tell me, please tell me that what I am thinking is not even close. I beg you, please don't tell me you are doing something in Mexico with drugs."

"Drugs?" Will begins to laugh. "Drugs?!"

"Seriously, Will," Jimmy said, feeling mocked, "what else could you be doing that makes that kind of money?"

"Drugs?" Will was in full, all out laughter.

"You're in Mexico, I know you speak Spanish and it makes sense to use a guy like you from a family like ours. No one would suspect a thing," reasoned Jimmy.

"Jimmy, I've got to hand it to you. I have forgotten how to laugh like that," Will said, patting his brother's chest. "Yes, we do have to talk and I'll explain everything. I need a good man on the outside—"

"What?"

"Just kidding," said Will. "I need you to see this. We'll be back in Dallas on Friday. Stay on the plane and we'll take a quick trip to the coast. I'll have you back Saturday afternoon. We won't miss a single bowl game. I promise."

"Anna can't come. Her parents arrive in Dallas on Saturday."

"Don't want her to come. This is just us two,, and don't mention this to a soul. This is strictly a Hoke brothers trip," warned Will

"Is this legal?" asked a sheepish Jimmy.

"So, is Anna pregnant?" asked Will.

"You're such an ass," replied Jimmy as he tried unsuccessfully to pull Will into a headlock.

***

The man who had watched the massive tower grow with the new construction, from a small boat floating on the Gulf, still had no idea what was going on. He had noticed the tugboat that had made its way out with lumber and other supplies. He knew that they had told him they were studying fish for the U.S. government and that they were students but something still did not add up.

In many cases, American students are kidnapped and held for ransom. College kids have parents who have money, but the international attention that would bring was always a concern. They hadn't been any problem or interfered with his activities in any way, but something still bothered him. Something wasn't right. And when he saw helicopters land, that seemed like a big expense for something like studying fish.

Turning to his driver, he commands him to start the boat and depart, "*Vamanos!*"

***

As the plane began to descend into the Dallas metroplex, Will looked down upon the skyline. He turned to Jimmy and asked if he still wanted to learn where the money came from. Once on the tarmac at Love Field, Will explained to the guys that since he still had the jet until Sunday morning so Jimmy and him were going to do some "bonding." They had all seen too much of each other in the past three days, so they were fine (even pleased) that Will was going away.

Jimmy, on the other hand, was doing his best to explain to Anna that he needed to be with Will and would be back ASAP on Sunday morning. "Look, you saw my brother's extravagance this week and I'm a little concerned. He's going to show me his business today."

"You're going to Mexico?" Anna asked (and why wouldn't she since the whole story of Mexico was all anyone ever heard).

"No, I'm only going to McAllen or somewhere nearby," Jimmy tried to assure her, but he wondered if she knew he was deceiving his future wife—this was no way to start a marriage.

"Well, when he told me about his time in Mexico, not everything added up," Anna said. "He's not being truthful with you."

"That is why I am going down there. I'll know if this is right or not. If you had a sister or brother who you were concerned for, you would try to help them, right?"

"Go, but, if you go across the border and get your head cut off by some Mafioso, don't come running to me."

"That would never happen," Jimmy promised her. "Because, when I met you I lost my head over you already. Get it? You get it?" Laughing, Jimmy tried to charm her with his humor.

"Yes, I get it. You are so dumb," Anna said trying not to laugh but failing. "Just go."

"And I remember that we are doing lunch at the W and then your parents at my folks that same night. See, I'm paying attention." Jimmy kissed Anna's forehead and smiled as he backed away towards the jet. "Love you."

***

"Heeey, congrats, John!" Agent Spivey called out on his cell. "You got your tax deduction for the year! What time did she get here?"

"*He* made it at 3:12 a.m. and I made it with just an hour to spare," said Agent Andrews. "It was like the moment we were airborne, I guess they began to call me, so when we hit North Carolina, I turned my phone on and had a dozen texts and calls."

"I thought you guys were told you were getting a girl."

"Yep, it was a surprise for us," said Andrews. "No offense, but why are you calling today?"

"Well, our friend in the Caymans emailed me."

"Trevor?"

"Yeah, did he email you, too?"

"Wouldn't know, I've kinda been occupied. What did he say?"

"Yeah, sorry for the call except to check in on you and your wife. Congrats, again!" said Spivey. "You do sound tired so I'll let you go."

"What did he say?"

"Well, I think he's trying to recant some things. He wants us to call him after New Year's Day."

"I'm definitely off until then, so it can wait," said Andrews. "Oh, and sorry about that Wisconsin game."

"Ahh, I knew you'd bring that up. You're not that tired."

"That was on auto-pilot, I am beat. We'll talk Wednesday," said Andrews. "In fact, why don't you reach out to Trevor before then, see what he has to say."

***

As the helicopter touched down, Jimmy looked out over the vast darkness and wondered about the safety of the oil rig. In December, the sun goes down in the Gulf before six. The vastness of where he was or what he could see would not be realized until morning.

"Well, you are either in the oil business or we're going fishing," said Jimmy.

"Step down the stairs here and turn right," ordered Will. "Walk into the first door you come to. I'll be in there in two minutes."

He could hear Will speaking to other people. He heard laughter and what sounded as if someone was offering gifts, he sat down and saw flat screen TVs, computers with several monitors and a world atlas on the wall. As he stood to inspect the flags that covered this wall, Will walked in and asked. "What do you think?"

"About what? Are you in the internet business?" Jimmy wearily asked.

"I guess you could say I am," replied Will. "The internet of personal finances or what some might call the lottery, we prefer to call it a raffle."

"Do explain."

"Well, it came to me one night after a Mavs game. I noticed a bartender pouring shots and I saw how each one had filled before he moved to the next glass. I imagined doing that with money and filling pots until one fills up and them moving to the next one. See, we are not a lottery. Actually, we are a raffle. In a raffle, there always is a winner and with this, you don't have to be present to win."

"Unbelievable. I've never heard of this," said Jimmy.

"Really? I'm hurt and disappointed. We do so much to market ourselves."

"Look, Will. We weren't raised this way. The lottery, or raffle or shots, or whatever the hell it is, is for the trailer park and Vegas types. We come from privilege," argued Jimmy.

"Not so!" demanded Will. "Our dad controls our trusts. He's forty-eight and if he lives another forty years, I'll be sixty-six! Sixty-six before I can touch my trust, bullshit on that!"

"Will, you never gave law school a try—"

"I didn't want to become a lawyer," yelled Will. "I never wanted to become dad!"

"Then what did you want to be? Dad will never allow you just to be a slacker."

"Slacker?" An angered Will said to Jimmy. His face was one of hurt but suddenly a smirk came to his face and he approached Jimmy and for a second he thought he was going to punch him. Instead, Will simply said, "Then slack this."

He turned on the and walked around the room as if the supreme commander of some international force. Pointing to the map on the wall, Will asked, "Notice how many small pins are located throughout the world? Want to count them?"

"What's your point, Will?" asked Jimmy, seeing the pins numbered in the thousands.

Will buzzed the next room, he leaned into the intercom and asked, "Anyone. How many to date winners do we have?"

"Twenty thousand two hundred and sixty-one," said a female voice.

"Numerically spell that out to me," said Will.

"Two, zero, zero, two, six one. Twenty thousand two hundred and sixty-one winners," she repeated.

"Thank you. Continue your fine work," Will said.

"OK, twenty thousand plus, that a lot of people," agreed Jimmy.

"No, young brother, that is 20,000 plus one million dollar winners of which, we *the house* withhold 8 percent. That is 80 grand each winner. Do the math. That alone is $1.6 billion dollars, divided by four. Any debit or bank fees are paid by them, not us. They take 1% and divide that up between five more random winners to keep them happy at $2,000 each." Will leaned back, savoring the moment. "Four little *slackers* from Dallas, Texas."

Attempting to absorb the enormity of it all, Jimmy offered a limp reply. "This can't be so."

"Oh, little brother, it gets even better. Every transaction, be it $10 or $1,000 is charged a small $1 'service transaction fee' per ten tickets which equals at least another $100,000. Every jackpot we clear $160,000." Will sat back in his chair and let the information sink in. "Questions?"

"How is this possible?" the astounded little brother asked.

"Jimmy, we are in international waters. This rig belonged to Charles's grandfather. It's been out of use since the '90s. So, being in international waters, who do we report to? No One! We simply provide a chance to win big money from the privacy and comfort of one's own computer without the expense of going to Vegas, Monaco, Macau or an Indian casino. No need to run to the local 7-11 to buy a lottery ticket. Our website is available in forty-two languages." He turned a monitor toward Jimmy to show him the live feed. Will added, "It's not QVC, it's MundoLottery.com and we have 20,000 millionaires to our credit." He paused, then said, "Well, 20,000 plus four very multi, multi-millionaires."

"You are crazy. This is a Ponzi scheme."

"Wrong again. We pay," said Will. "Once we confirm the winning ticket, we call or we email the winner. We give them three options to receive their money. Wired direct to the personal account of their own choosing. Taxes will have to be paid. Two, certified check from a Cayman bank. Taxes will have to be paid. Three, we help them set up a Cayman or Swiss account. Swiss accounts are a little harder now, mind you, but, still no taxes. Now little brother, which do you think the people go for?"

"So each pin represents a winner?" Jimmy asked fighting to not appear too impressed.

"All continents. All seven billion people can play," Will continued to make his case. "We average 4.3 winners per hour, 24 hours a day, because the world never sleeps, 365 days a year and that is only because we started in April. At this rate we'll gross over $37 billion dollars next year with each of us earning around $1.6 billion dollars. That's each. Cash. Not stock."

"Unreal," Jimmy offered his first note of approval.

"Every night, we download the data, the winners, account numbers of winners and our own personal accounts onto this one 4 Gigabyte thumb drive." Will held up the device for Jimmy to inspect. "You might say that this little device holds all the money, and all the secrets."

"Will, I don't know what to say. I don't know whether to be impressed or pissed that you didn't include me," said Jimmy.

"Ah, there are drawbacks. We do have to operate with total anonymity. We can't be back home doing this, we have to travel when we go to Europe without frequent flyer numbers or we have to rent a jet, we miss home games . . . oops, that reminds me, I promised you wouldn't miss a bowl game." Will turned on the TV and began searching for the game. "Now we do live an isolated, remote existence. Chuck's woman gave up on him and he kinda freaked on us a little."

"You have managed to circumvent the system. Unbelievable," Jimmy repeated.

"We do live in a little fear because we can't hire the security we probably should have because that would alert anyone out here in the Gulf that something was up. I have installed an emergency chute in case we need to make a break for it. We have a speed boat docked below. We own a *fishing* boat in Corpus that operates as a business, for any tax purposes, I'm buying a cruise boat for the same—"

"And the kind of money to get into any club in West Hollywood."

"Oh, yeah. About that that. I was pretty drunk when I bought that club."

"You bought it?!"

"Yeah, I was pissed that we couldn't get in. I bought it just to fire that bouncer."

"But, you didn't?" asked Jimmy.

"No, I guess I didn't." He leaned back and ran his hands thru his hair, "What am I going to do with a $2 million club that I can't enjoy? Not being there, you know the managers are going to rape the profits from there."

"How did you come up with $2 million on the spot?" Jimmy asked. "Tell me you didn't have two million in cash on you there."

"No," insisted Will, "I used a debit card."

"A debit card?"

Laughter broke out between the two of them, they rolled in their chairs laughing at the thought of using a debit card to purchase something like a nightclub.

"Is that even possible? I would think that it wouldn't clear. Who keeps $2 million dollars in a checking account?!"

They continued to laugh at the insanity of it all. The money. The ease to buy something and the frivolous spending that it was.

"Seriously Jimmy," said Will leaning into Jimmy. "It's good that you know and I feel a huge weight is off me, but you must never, I mean never, tell anyone, especially Anna."

"Done."

"Now, little brother, let me show you around *The Island*."

***

The phone rang at the Hoke home. Cricket answered expecting it to be for her but instead she walked the phone to her father. "It's for you. It's a 310 number."

Will Sr. took the phone and said, "Hello, this is Will."

Standing by with a half-curious interest, Cricket listened to the one-sided conversation.

"Do what?" said her father. "No, I did not buy a club." "No honey, I'm a forty-eight-year old married lawyer and my wife probably wouldn't go for that."

"Yes, I am Will Hoke but I did not buy a club. All right, goodbye."

He handed the phone back to Cricket.

"That was odd. Some Hollywood reporter asking if I bought a nightclub in West Hollywood a couple of days ago," he said. "Your brother's not out in LA trying to buy a club is he?"

His comments were more for personal amusement rather than considering the possibility that his wayward son could have the funds to buy a club. He did, after all, control the purse strings.

Cricket agreed that it was odd and walked upstairs to her room and grabbed her cell phone to call Will, but it went straight to voicemail. She tried to call Jimmy but got the same results. Then tried Anna and was surprised to hear the phone ring.

"Anna, Cricket. Is Jimmy with you? Can I speak with him?"

"No, he and Will took the plane down to McAllen for the projects that Will does," Anna said. "Why? Is something wrong?"

"No. Nothing wrong," Cricket said, then offered, "Someone just called the house asking for Will, but Dad took the call. They wanted to know if he bought a club in Los Angeles. What happened out there?"

"No, it was a wild time, a little wilder than I would like," Anna confessed. "Your brothers had fun."

"It was an odd call. Dad just said 'no, I didn't buy a club in LA,' but they don't about Junior and Dad doesn't know you guys went out there."

"That is odd, but I will tell you this, we went to one of those clubs where all the Hollywood types go to, and this doorman wouldn't let us in but Will paid the manager something and got us all in. Your brother was throwing money around like a billionaire."

"Jimmy did?" asked Cricket.

"No, Will was," said Anna.

"Was it the Viper Room?" Cricket asked.

"The what room?" Anna asked.

"The Viper Room, it's a big deal, but now I'm curious where you went. Did you see any famous people?"

"Yes, Jimmy saw someone he said he was always infatuated with ever since he was a little boy. She was in a children's show," Anna laughed. "She is grown up now and trying to do music, or something."

"Yes, I know who you are talking about," laughing at her brother. "Did he talk to her?"

"No, so I went up to her and told her 'my fiancé has always had a thing for you, but you had better hurry while he is still on the market,'" Anna laughed.

"You didn't," challenged Cricket.

"Oh, yes I did," said Anna continuing to laugh.

"What did she say?"

"Oh, she said something like 'I don't need more men' or something like that, but to see the look on your brother's face."

"I would have loved to!"

"For once your brother had no comeback. Ask him about it, I am sure he will tell you how cool he was. Don't believe it."

"I'm mad that I didn't go now," said Cricket.

"Well, it was wild like I said. Will had a new girl with him," Anna revealed. "Some girl from SMU he said he knew before."

"When was the last you spoke with Jimmy?"

"He called me around 5 when I was at the airport waiting on my parents. We had a bad connection."

"Your parents? Forgot about that. So, I get to see them here tomorrow night. That ought to be fun. Let me let you go then. See ya tomorrow."

Cricket hung up the phone and her curiosity got the better of her. She grabbed her laptop and began to search for news in Hollywood about clubs changing ownership.

***

"This is the Theater Room. Here we have movies every night and see, we have our own popcorn machine and soda fountain. Of course, we catch all the games we can off the satellite . . . we try to keep everyone happy."

"How did you get this set up for satellite?"

"That was a little challenge," admitted Will. "We met some guy in Corpus and he bragged that he could get anything done and he did. We get it illegally, but we can and would like to pay, just how to do it is a problem. Not like we have a mailbox downstairs or address for that matter."

They continued walking thru the massive rig, down past the new tennis court and weight room. Will pointed to the door.

"See that handle? That is in case of an emergency. It is a slide that goes down to the water. In case of hurricane or—"

"Pirate attack?" asked Jimmy.

"Don't laugh. It's not ever far from my mind," admitted Will. "Come here and let me show something."

He opened a cabinet that housed a small arsenal, Will handed Jimmy a tactical rifle. Jimmy held it and peered down the barrel into the darkness.

"That is an M15 with 30 rounds of .223," Will explained. "That's the same size as Dad's hunting rifle but much, much more badass."

"Nice, huh?" asked Jimmy.

"It'll make you want to smoke a cigarette afterwards," said Will who reached in his pocket and pulled out two cigars, handing one to Jimmy. "In fact, here ya go."

"Cuban cigars, full auto assault rifles, tax evasion. Wow man, our parents would be so proud," smirked Jimmy. "When is this going to end? You can't do this forever."

"Glad you asked there, Jimmy." Will responded. "Once, I hit a billion or so in cash, for each of us, we're, done."

Will put the M15 away and they walked back to the office where Will sat down at his desk and held his palms out as if to asking for more questions.

"And when will that be? When will you be done?"

"Could be as soon as April," Will predicted. "That means that we did it in a year. A year, Jimmy and I'll never have to put up with any BS from Dad, or anyone."

"How will you describe your sudden wealth?"

"Foreign investors," Will stated firmly.

"So, what are you worth now?" Jimmy asked. "How close are you?"

"I don't know," Will turned the computer monitor to face Jimmy, "why don't you tell me? There at the bottom."

Leaning into the screen, Jimmy began to read aloud, "What's this, seven hundred, forty-seven million? Eight hun—"

"That's enough," interrupted Will. "The rest are just smaller numbers."

"You have 747 million in cash?!" Jimmy asked shaking his head in disbelief. "So you've just got everything figured out there, brother. Everything."

"By the way, I alone have made about 80 grand since we got here," Will said, almost as if he was rubbing it in. "Well, we've had two winners in the last 25 minutes. Just sayin'."

Discovery

"No, Will is not here," said Mrs. Hoke. "He's gone for a jog and should be back around 11. Who may I say is calling?" She listened a while more and added. "Oh, well I don't think you have the right Will. We are, of course, in Dallas."

At that point, Cricket offered to take the call from her mother. Since she was busy planning for Jimmy's future in-laws later that night, she was thrilled to be relieved of the call.

"Hi, this is Cricket. Can I help you?" Cricket moved away from her Mom and lowered her voice, suspecting something was at play here.

"Yes, Cricket. My name is Brenda Raines and I'm with an industry magazine for the nightlife in Los Angeles. On Thursday night, a twenty-six year old man named William Hoke who claimed to be from Dallas, bought the famed Authority Bar and paid for it in cash. This was the only number that was working listed to a William Hoke. Do you know this William Hoke?"

"William Hoke is my dad, but I might . . . ," she tried to think of some way to stall for now, "Well, why don't you give me your number and I can call you back? Can I use the 323 number? . . . Your cell . . . Great, will call you back."

She hung up and stood there holding the phone in her hand. Not knowing who to call or even where Will was, she asked her Mom when lunch was being served.

"You are on your own today," she said, "I'm getting ready for everyone tonight."

"Will Junior be here?" Cricket asked.

"Of course."

She tried Will's cell phone but 400 miles away, he was seated on the plane and had just turned his phone off. She left no message.

Her father entered the kitchen from the back door and Mrs. Hoke informed him that he just missed a call from California. "Who is calling you from there at this time of morning?" she asked.

"I don't know but that is second time they've called," he said. Taking the phone from Cricket, he checked the Caller ID button and read (323) 389- . . . . "Yesterday, was a 310 number. I have no idea what's up."

***

Stepping off the plane, Will's phone rang the minute he turned it on.

"Hello, Cricket. Skipping church today?"

"Will. What this about you buying a nightclub in LA?" she inquired.

"Who said anything about that?" He asked. Holding the phone low and cupping it in his palms, he angrily asked Jimmy. "Did you tell Cricket about the club?!"

"No, I've not spoken to her since, well, since we left for LA."

"Cricket, where'd you hear about that?" asked Will.

"So, it's true? Cool."

"No!" Will asserted. "Who's saying that I did. Have you spoken with Robert or Stu?"

"No, reporters from an LA magazine called the house. Twice." she confided. "They thought it was Dad but he was confused and blew them off. He doesn't even know you went to LA."

"Hold on, Cricket. I'm here at Love Field and will be at the house within 30 minutes. Does Mom have lunch made?"

"No, she's preparing for Anna's family tonight."

"Then meet me at Lucky's on Oak Lawn for lunch. OK?" He warned, "Say nothing to no one."

Will informed Jimmy that someone from LA had been calling asking questions and now Cricket knew about the club.

"Someone called the house from LA about you buying the club?" Jimmy asked.

"Yeah, and Cricket thinks it's 'cool'."

"She would," Jimmy agreed. "You'll have to drop me off at Anna's."

***

That night at the Hoke house on Beverly Avenue, Anna and her family were greeted at the door by Mr. and Mrs. Hoke. The pleasantries were exchanged and Will Sr. couldn't help but notice the height difference between Anna's parents. The father so short and the mother so tall.

Inviting them into the living room, they were all seated. The typical awkward introductions were made along with the typical compliments like "you have a lovely home" and that moment of silence after the host and guest speak at the same time.

Will sat back and enjoyed the tension. He tried to catch a glimpse of Jimmy whenever he could in hopes of making him feel awkward. Hey, it's what brothers do, he thought. He thought of how uncomfortable Jimmy looked and yet, how comfortable, attractive and at ease Anna was. Oh gosh, did he have a crush on his brother's fiancé? No, he simply wanted the best for him. He was glad that the happiness that he had with Karina wasn't stolen from him by the same man he sat across from in this very room. Watching him, he couldn't help wonder why this was different. He had always thought it was that because Karina was Hispanic but here was Anna direct from Mexico City. It seemed that his father was almost trying too hard. He had never seen this in him before. "Why now?" he wondered.

It was great that Cricket and Anna were quickly becoming friends. In fact, they were the two most at ease in the room, well and then there was Will. He was at ease and why wouldn't he be. He wasn't trying to impress anyone and he knew that he had more money than anyone else in the room. He was damn near a billionaire—in just a few months he would be—but this was about his brother and right now Jimmy needed him and charm was Will's ticket.

"Mr. Reynoso, what do you do?" asked Will.

"I work for Banco Nationale," stated Reynoso with a pleasant enough smile.

"Daddy is being modest," explained Anna, "He is the Senior Vice President over all of Mexico State."

"We'll that's better than being VP over Tlaxcala State," shot Will.

"Will, that is so rude," his mother reprimanded him then turned to the Reynosos to apologize, "Please, accept our apologies for the rudeness and immaturity of our eldest son."

From the look on his face, Mr. Reynoso was not amused and not used to such candor thrown his direction, for he was a very powerful man. A man who could ride the political turmoil of Mexico from candidates and party affiliations, a man who could well afford to send his daughter to the best U.S. universities. Someone whose phone calls were eagerly accepted. A man whose friendship is coveted.

"Mom, Tlaxcala is the smallest state in Mexico. It is the, uh, Rhode Island of Mexico," Will carefully explained. "We are all very impressed with Anna and it would reason that she represents her family well, too. Obviously, we were right."

You could have heard a pin drop in Austin because no one knew if this was sufficient enough to regain any lost favor. A small grin from Mr. Reynoso still did not make clear if all was forgiven. The look on Jimmy's face said things were not going so well, so Will made one more attempt.

"*Senor y Senora Reynoso, perdone por favor mi tentativa de facilitar la tensión con una mala broma. Amamos a Anna e intentaba solamente poner cada uno en la facilidad,*" Will paused and waited for his Spanish to resonate, then continued, "*Soy su cuñado futuro y cuando se casan, todos seremos familia. Ella está consiguiendo al buen hermano, Jimmy. Y, y ninguin falta de respeto significado hacia Tlaxcala.*"

"*Claro,*" said Reynoso. Finally showing a look of ease and approval, he stood up and approached Will with a faint smile, "And here I was all set to watch Jimmy with my daughter but this one here, this is the one I need to watch more."

"Daddy, Will has worked extensively in Mexico helping some communities in *El Norte,*" Anna said, explaining both Will and his Spanish abilities in one sentence.

Cricket tried her hand at easing any remaining tension, "Do you have a date set?"

"No, Jimmy and I haven't set a date," Anna said. "All this has been so fast."

"A little fast, I guess," said Reynoso, who returned his attention to Will. "And now just what do you do Will?"

"I work with foreign investors," Will said looking over at his father to gauge his reaction. "I take their money to invest."

"Oh then, perhaps you would like to invest some of those funds into the Mexican banks someday," offered Reynoso.

Will looked for approval from Jimmy, only to catch a short look of no. Laughing to himself for both saving the day and making Jimmy squirm. "We'll have to see, Mr. Reynoso," Will said, hoping to get a "call me Faustino" reply. Getting no such reply, he asked, "So, how's my brother doing with you, Mr. Reynoso?"

"Ah, Jimmy is a fine man," Reynoso said. "I told you that the day you asked my permission to marry Anna, right Jimmy?"

"You asked?" a shocked Anna asked Jimmy. "When did you do that?"

"When they came up for Thanksgiving," said Jimmy. "You and your mom were out shopping."

"Wow, to be surprised like that," Anna said. "You know, that was a concern when you asked me because in the back of my mind I kept thinking that my father will be disappointed you didn't ask."

"So you thought that and still accepted his proposal?" her father asked. Turning to Mr. & Mrs. Hoke, he said, "These kids only think of themselves, not their parents."

"Well, Mr. Reynoso," said Will Sr., "I am delighted that you have graciously accepted our son. I hope that I can be so gracious and that *my* daughter makes an equally smart choice when she decides to marry."

"And call me Faustino," said Reynoso.

"Dad, you have never approved of any guy I've dated," said Cricket.

"True," said Will Sr., "but, in truth they have all been unworthy."

"When I was a young man in college, my girlfriend's father was very disapproving. And he was not good at hiding it," said Reynoso. "He told me that I was unworthy of his daughter and that I was only marrying her for *his* money."

"Well, looks like you did better anyway in the long run." Will Sr. said extending his hand in the direction Anna's mother in the form of a compliment.

"Oh no. He was unworthy and only after the money," said Mrs. Reynoso to a stunned room. "But, I married him anyway."

"I never tire of that joke," said Reynoso. "But seriously, I promised I would not want to do that to anyone, especially with Jimmy." He added an approving look towards his future son-in-law. "By the way, how was your time in Los Angeles?"

Suddenly, it was as if the room itself cringed. Jimmy, Cricket and Will never imagined that this was how their father would learn about the trip to LA. Will felt the glaring stare of his father upon him, he dared not look in that direction.

Continuing, Reynoso said directly to Mrs. Hoke, "We went to Los Angeles last about five years ago. One night we are eating at this one restaurant and I hear something in Castilian and I look to see who it is, and it is Antonio Banderas."

"Oh, yes!" added an excited Mrs. Reynoso, "he is so beautiful."

"Yes, and so you have said many times," continued Reynoso. "Anyway Anna's mother gets up and approaches the table. I was so embarrassed. Anna your mother left me at the table for Antonio Banderas!"

"He tells that story as if I acted like a school girl," Mrs. Reynoso said laughing, dismissing his accusation.

"You did," he declared. "Needless to say that, now we avoid Los Angeles."

Will's mom got caught up in the humor of the story and offered, "Yes, well Jimmy's father has always been enamored with that woman from that movie *The Outsiders*. Oh, my gosh what is her name?" Thinking for a second, she said, "Diane Lane."

"Bonnie, you can never remember any detail about a single movie but you can remember her name," said Will Sr.

"That's funny, Dad," said Cricket. "I'd never heard that one before."

Seizing the light moment, Will turned to face his dad but the jig was up. The look his father gave him told Will that he knew all about the club in LA.

Will's father leaned in and whispered, "Boy, we need to talk later." Will hadn't been called boy since, well he couldn't remember and it didn't feel good now. He turned to Reynoso and asked if anyone wanted another round of drinks. Will wanted to be anywhere now, anywhere but in the same room as his Dad.

***

Upon closing the door, after the two families had said their goodbyes, Bonnie turned and said, "Well, I think that went quite well."

"Yes, he's a nice looking gentleman, Anna's Dad," said Cricket. "I told you that before."

Will used this simple chatter as cover, and started making his exit from the house. He was halted before making his escape by his father's voice, "Not so fast, son."

Will spun around and came face to face with his father. Eye contact was imminent and Will prepared for interrogation. "Son, why am I getting calls from LA reporters about buying a nightclub in LA?" His questions were direct and did not offer any wiggle room. The only two options would be to lie or tell the truth. Before Will could speak, he was hit with more questions. "Does it have anything to do with you being in LA this week and that we share the same name?"

"No biggie. Yes, I was in LA," said Will.

"Then, what's this about a nightclub, Will?" asked his Dad. "Seriously, what a sleazy business to get into."

"It was some foreign investors who could not own property in the U.S. some additional tax issue, so I was paid to have my name as owner." Will opted for lying. "It was a simple business deal. You should be proud."

"Son, we are not flashy people. We are not like the Schlendel family here. It is a citywide joke the way they have their kids in every magazine in town. We are not trying to be Kardashian wannabees!"

"Yeah, I always thought that was pretty needy," agreed Will.

"Will, I have always wanted our family to represent a respect that you don't get with something as sleazy as a nightclub and all the implications that brings."

"Like what?"

"Son, don't be stupid."

"Dad, it is a very exclusive club," Will justified. "Diane Lane probably went there in her younger days."

"Son, don't get smart with me," his father snapped. "Look, you go off to Mexico, then show up months later with very expensive gifts for everyone and your hands are not those of a man working a shovel or whatever the hell you claim to be doing down there."

Sensing his lie might be exposed, Will offered a simple explanation. "Dad, once again, I am more the manager there and others do the manual work."

"Just being down there keeps your mother up at night! We never know when the phone rings at night if it is someone informing us that you're dead or kidnapped! Do you know that if one of those Mexican gangs found out the money you come from, you'd be a hostage within minutes!!"

"Dad don't worry. From now on, I'm staying stateside. You're right. It is getting too bad down there."

"Son, are you mixed up with drug money down there? That's what this looks like to me, and why the hell else would someone pay you instead of an attorney or form some business entity? And clubs are notorious for laundering money."

Will began thinking that maybe his lie wasn't so great after all. "You're right. I hadn't considered that. I simply saw an opportunity to make money."

"Son, you have been a very big disappointment to me."

"OK, daddy. What do you want from me? To be successful, right?"

"Respectably successful," his father said. "Have a professional career. Marry right. Just be respectable."

Suddenly a fury awoke within Will, seeing Karina it all came rushing back in his mind. That long repressed hurt that suddenly returned when Jimmy introduced Anna. The one love of his life has been lost because of the man he was now being interrogated by.

"Marry right?" Will asked. "Like Jimmy?"

"Yes. Anna is a very fine girl. She comes from a well-respected family," his father reasoned. "Cricket had known her for some time before Jimmy ever met her. That was good enough for me."

"Unlike Karina," Will shot back.

"Son, Karina was a fine and very beautiful girl," Will's father offered, "but she would have had a hard time adjusting to this lifestyle. She did very well to get a scholarship and without that she never would have come here, and did you know she had a brother in prison?"

"Actually, I did," Will said. "She never spoke of him. I only learned of him because I saw a photo at her home and asked who he was. She was ashamed of him and I don't blame her. Let me ask you, if Anna came from the same humble means, would you feel about her like you did Karina? Would you ruin with Jimmy what you ruined with me?"

"Son, I only wanted the best for you."

"Dad, everyone on campus wanted what I had in her."

"I bet they did," was his father's tart reply.

"You will be picking yourself off the floor if you ever say something like that about her again," Will calmly threatened.

"Son, I'm just saying that she was an attractive poor girl and some girls use that to get a guy like you."

"You so don't even know," Will said. "And, by the way, am I respectable?"

"Yes. Yes, you are," said his father.

"Well, then. I am wildly successful, too," Will confessed, expanding his arms out. "Then, I guess *I am* all you want me to be and you don't even have a clue."

"What's that supposed to mean?" his father shot back.

"It means that I am outta here." Walking past his mom who had been standing in the doorway the whole time, Will mumbled, "Goodnight, Mom."

His mom gave a quick kiss and watched Will leave. She turned to Will Sr. and asked "Well, what do you think that meant?"

"Don't know what he's into, honey," Will Sr. said, "but, I know how to find out."

Return to The Island

As the helicopter landed, the foursome stepped out and were greeted by all of the workers. This was odd because never before had they been met like this.

"We brought no gifts," offered Stu.

"No, it's not about that," said one of the girls. "Did you see the boat?"

"What boat?" asked Robert.

"That one," she said, pointing out to the sea. "It just showed up this morning and circled us. It's just creepy."

"Well, how close has it come to the rig?" asked Charles.

"Maybe, two hundred yards," offered a young male.

"Did you use the binoculars?" asked Stu.

"Yes, but they were too far away."

"Did you use the telescope?" asked Robert.

"No. It is locked your cave."

"Well, everyone go back inside. We look paranoid gathered like this," said Stu.

"Leave it up there," ordered Will. "I don't want them to see me looking." As he peered thru the binoculars, he asked the surrounding workers, "How have you guys been?"

"Fine, since we just saw you just two days ago," said one of the workers.

Will had slipped up by asking that question, he had not informed the guys that his brother Jimmy was aware of their venture and had been on *The Island* just days prior.

"What?" asked Charles.

"I called out here to check supplies," said Will. Attempting to drop the questioning, he reported, "I see the boat and on the side it says *pesca* which is Spanish for fishing. You guys are scared of a fishing boat."

"Well, why did it circle us?" the girl asked.

"Dunno," said Will, "but I guess it's good to be just a little paranoid."

***

In a well-manicured office, the phone rang and the man behind the desk answered, "David Fairfield."

"Yes, Mr. Hoke, I was told to expect your call. Who are we checking on? Um, huh. Can you give full names? Any dates of birth?" He scribbled old school on a note pad while continuing to ask questions. "What are you looking for, concerns? Can you supply me with a social security number? No problem, I can get that. How soon do you need this? OK, then. I'll be away until the 20th or so, give me a couple of weeks then, I'll let you know where I am. You have a good day, Mr. Hoke."

***

"Gentlemen, I hope you had a good Christmas and New Year," the Director said as he sat down. "Although, I expected very little from your trip and am pretty sure it was wasted money, I'll ask anyways, so how were the Caymans?"

"Well actually, sir, much better than Switzerland," reported Andrews.

"Really? Surprising, since we have no treaty with them. My sending you was strictly a knee-jerk reaction due to the Swiss being less than helpful. So what did the banks say?"

"Well, that's the funny part. The banks were of no help," said Andrews, "but we met an actual lottery winner and he began to talk."

"John here used a great strategy to get him to talk," Spivey popped in.

"That's nothing important," said Andrews. "We engaged a young twenty-three year old Cayman national there who had won a million dollar jackpot."

"How much did he pay to play?" asked the Director.

"He didn't," said Spivey. "He worked as a waiter at a press conference when they invited the world media there back in September. Not only was he paid, each media reporter, cameraman, newspaper writer as well as waiters and busboys got a $500 Visa card to play. He said after work he went home and played immediately."

"So he went from being a $10 an hour waiter to millionaire with the swipe of a Visa card, a card he didn't even pay for?"

"Yes, basically," said Andrews. "He did indicate that he thinks the people behind the lottery site are from the U.S. He said there were three men present at the press conference, but he never saw their faces. He said word on the street was that they were from Florida or Texas possibly, due to their quick access to the Caymans. It is rumored that they visit quite often."

"But they don't operate in any of the Caribbean islands because those countries would have their hands out for money all the time," said the Director. "Right?"

"We believe they do have some business filings in Panama," said Andrews.

"Any luck in tracing their satellite feeds?" asked the Director.

"None, so we assume they must be in a remote location," said Spivey. "Is it possible that they are doing this from a boat?"

"Then wouldn't the webcam be rocking or something?" inquired Andrews, who took the comment to be a foolish one.

"Not if they were on an ocean liner or cruise ship," reasoned Spivey.

The Director reached for his phone. In 4 digits, he had his party. "Wilson, are you available? Then come down the hall." He hung up and said, "Boys, I sent you down there because I knew that the Swiss would speak with the Caymans and I wanted to throw a little fear into them. You getting the young man to speak, is a big plus. Oh and, congratulations on your baby girl there, Andrews."

"It was a boy, sir," Andrews corrected.

"Whatever." Turning his focus to Wilson who had just walked into the room, he asked, "Wilson, any luck locating those signals regarding our offshore lottery?"

"Yes sir. We traced the signals out into the Gulf of Mexico," she said. "We have known it to be operating in and around the Gulf since Christmas Day."

"See, I thought it might be a ship," Spivey said, feeling vindicated.

"No," Wilson countered. "Not a ship. Now it does float, but we theorize it might be an oil rig, at least the signal is bouncing off a rig."

The Director thought about how obvious it was, right under their noses. "An oil rig." He crossed his arms and repeated, "A damn oil rig."

***

"Surprise! Old school jamming." Will announced as he entered the breakfast room on the rig. He turned on the stereo and filled the room with the heavy metal classic "Crazy Train." How appropriate he thought.

"Surprise for what?" demanded Charles.

"Yeah, Will. You're full of them," said Stu.

"Look. I explained that I had to tell Jimmy. We need someone on the outside to know things in case of . . ." Will trailed off because the next words might not be so pleasant.

"In case of what?" demanded Robert.

"Ooh, tough crowd," said Will. "Look. None of you have close brothers and we can't tell sisters, friends or, fathers—understand?"

"All I can say is the more people that know, the more it can get out," argued Stu. "Loose lips, sink ships."

"Guys. You are killing my surprise!" demanded Will. "In two weeks, we are going home to Dallas. There is a party and since it's close enough to you guys' birthdays," he motioned to Robert and Charles, who grew up celebrating their birthdays two days apart, "we'll have to make it about that, too. My treat."

"Then, let's do it," said Stu. "Who is going to be there?"

"Everyone," he said. "And bring your passports."

At that moment, a young worker stuck her head in the room. "Will, I was told to tell you that we topped 23,000 last night at 5:21 a.m., or this morning at 5:21."

"Thanks Lisa," Will said, turning back to the guys. "Those Christmas gift cards paid off big, and not all have been redeemed. Life is good."

"When do we leave for home?" asked Charles.

"On the 26th. And each of you can invite 40 people. I'll need names," Will said as he exited the room.

***

Within the offices of the IRS, a special meeting had been called and everyone was in the conference room watching a video. The Director, Andrews, Spivey and Wilson were in attendance as were several others who had been brought in on the investigation. They were there to observe and hopefully pick up anything the previous investigators might have missed from the Mundo Lottery webcast.

"This is like watching the grass grow," whispered a junior agent, causing others to grin.

The Director stepped forward, paused the video, and addressed the group. "People, many of you might be aware of a worldwide, *illegal* website operated by a small group of individuals whom we believe to be U.S. citizens. Since April, this website has been offering a raffle-type scheme to anyone with a debit or credit card and access to the internet. Even a phone can access this site. We now know that this operation takes place somewhere in the Gulf of Mexico. Since the webcam never shows their faces and the clothing is nondescript it makes it hard to ID—Yes, Payne," he paused briefly take a question.

"If they are out in international waters, how do we have jurisdiction?"

"He just said that they are probably U.S. citizens," said a sarcastic colleague seated next to him.

"Their website is hosted out of Panama, so it's not like we can shut it down," Spivey added.

Continuing, Payne reasoned, "Well, if they are in another country, and *if* they are in international waters, then they are not breaking any U.S. laws."

Some of Payne's colleagues intervened attempting to get him to stop questioning the Director, but the Director cut them off. "Let him speak. I want everyone who works under me to have conviction in their heart. Continue Payne."

"Well, we assume they have not filed taxes for this past year? But since we don't even know who they are, how can we know if they filed taxes or not?"

Now the Director was growing irritated and thinking that maybe he should have let Payne's colleagues silence him. "People for the next two weeks, you will work in shifts and monitor this feed twenty-four hours a day I want you to watch for any clue, any face that might appear, any clothing that might turn out to be a regional piece, any jewelry that might provide us with an identity." Motioning to Andrews, he asked if he had anything else to add.

"From what we have gathered this site has pulled in at least $16 billion, that's billion with a **B**. Of that we estimate they have pocketed somewhere between $1.3 and $2.6 billion." Andrews relished his new approval from the Director and his willingness to allow him to speak. He chose his words cautiously. "People, aside from being able to buy a $10 domain to operate an illegal website, appearing on every continent in over 40 languages, they have no product to produce, and very little overhead. It clearly states on their website that they will be educating winners on how to shelter their money in Cayman and Swiss banks and thereby sheltering taxable income from their governments. And no one is above the law."

***

Sitting before a computer monitor, a young Middle Eastern man of eighteen years watched the jackpot filling up, fascinated by the possibility of winning such a windfall. He read the rules and called out to a friend in the room to whom he explained about the site, the winners, and their chances of winning. They debated the merits and possibilities. At this stage, the jackpot was low.

Their surroundings would lead one to believe that they lacked the financial means to even take a chance, but entering the numbers off a credit card, they were in the game.

Then panic set in. In his confusion of converting Dinar's into Dollars he had hit too many zeros! Now the jackpot was nearly full and they were in the game for $600,000! They would be killed if this loss of money were to be found out! This money was for funding terror cells and they had used it in a game of chance.

They sat in fear and then began to curse at one anther.

San Juan

Touching down in Dallas, the foursome was met by Jimmy, Anna and Cricket.

"Why did you get a van?" asked Will.

"Cricket brought some of her friends from school," said Jimmy. "They are still in the van."

"Happy birthday, guys!" Cricket said as she hugged Charles and Robert. "I heard I missed a wild time in LA."

"Yeah, well we'll have to make up for that," promised Charles. "So, where are we going?"

"Hey, sis-in-law, Anna, how's my baby bro doing?" Will asked, as he gave her a hug.

"Fine," said Anna.

"How are you parents?" Will asked.

"They are doing well," she said. "Daddy really liked you, Will."

"See there, brother," laughed Will with an evil taunt. "If you ever mess up, I'm there."

"Oh, he loves Jimmy," said Anna. "He's the son he never had."

"Then you really can't marry being brother and sister," said Will.

"Will, you are so *malo*," said Anna.

"Did you bring it?" Will asked Jimmy, who nodded a quick affirmative. "Then Charles, first, go get the champagne out of the van."

"Champagne?" Charles asked with a disgusted look. "I'm a man. Beer me, please."

"Just go get it," pleaded Will. "It's pretty cold standing here."

Charles ran off to the van while the others waited and watched.

"You did a good thing, Will," said Anna.

"Not if they reject each other," said Will. "Then, I'm up *rio de caca* with Charles for doing it."

"It was a gamble," said Jimmy.

"Did everyone bring their passport?" asked Will. Pulling Jimmy aside, Will leaned in and quietly asked "How are you explaining all this to Anna?"

"I plan to stick with the foreign investor theory," said Jimmy. "It is true, sorta."

They watched as Charles and Cindy embraced on the tarmac. They kissed and tried to talk between hugs. It had worked. Will, the Matchmaker.

"I guess you did do a good thing," said Anna. "Are you going to be solo on this trip?"

"I don't know. Haven't heard from Holly," said Will.

"OK, enough of this crap, where is this party?" complained Robert.

"It starts over there," Will said, pointing towards a 727. "It starts there in about ten minutes!"

"Where are we going?" asked Stu.

"Why do you care? It's not your birthday," said Robert.

"Will said to invite 40 people and I invited mostly dudes!" moaned Stu.

"Trust me. We will all do well this weekend," advised Will. "One more time, did everyone bring their passports?!" He waited until they had all given an affirmative answer, then ordered, "Now get your ass on the plane!"

Will gathered Robert and Charles (after all this was in honor of their birthdays) and ushered them onto the plane to the cheers of "Surprise!!"

"For me?" asked a shocked Charles. "I'll admit, you got me! Where are we going?"

"We only have enough gas for San Juan," answered Will.

"San Juan, should have got a bigger plane!" shot Robert.

"Hey, watch it. I haven't paid for your surprise yet," said Will.

"Will, you don't owe me a thing," said Robert. "Now, close those doors and let's go!"

As he sat down, Robert looked down the aisle seeing many familiar faces, then concentrated on one face in particular. A little confused, Robert leaned back towards Will and asked, "What is Zane French doing on this plane?"

"That's Charles' surprise. You know Zane's his favorite singer," said Will. "I don't think Charles has even noticed him, yet."

"Is he playing?" asked Robert.

"Of course, his band is back there somewhere," said Will. At that point, Robert jumped up and started heading towards the back. "We're about to take off. Where are you going?"

"It's my birthday, too," said an animated Robert, "so Tracy Grace must be on this flight!"

"Sit down, man, yours is coming soon enough. Nice try, though."

Robert and Will toasted with beers. "To you, Will," said Robert.

"No, to *The Money Island*," corrected Will.

***

Back at the small shell of an apartment, two Middle Eastern men did not have to wait long for the *pot* to reach one million. It did that soon after they had made their error and purchased 600,000 tickets instead of 600. But then as they waited for the confirmation of the winner, time seemed to stop. The moments went by slower than either had ever experience before.

Suddenly the numbers appeared, and they scrambled in a nervous attempt to decipher their fate. Then they hear the familiar ding which signaled the arrival of email. The subject line read: ATTENTION MUNDO LOTTERY WINNER!!

They had won! They stood in jubilation, danced and hugged. They bounced and sang. They had won and they would live!

***

Andrews felt as though he was losing the opportunity he had been given. So far, he had been given two foreign trips, a new position and subordinates, yet he had no names, no location, no proof.

"So what are you telling me here, Andrews?" asked the Director.

"Well, with a clear intent to hide their identities since Day One they have worn very bland, white t-shirts and jeans," Andrews began. "No wedding bands, so we assume they are young and unmarried, no definitive music or radio can be overheard on the webcam. We only hear voices when they are congratulating the winners. They have no product or even a service to sell, it is just a numbers game. A game of luck."

"I don't get it, Andrews," opined the Director. "We're not dealing with a governmental agency here. These people had to be very well off to begin with, just the start up cost alone would have stopped most people. Do you agree?"

"Yes sir, but if they have that much money already, then why do something like this?" asked Andrews. "Why not just have fun with the money they already had?"

"Perhaps they only have the money for a short time?" wondered the Director.

"Or, what if they lived like they had money but aren't eligible to get it for a while?" asked Andrews. "Like kids with money. Trust fund kids."

Agent Spivey walked in with a DVD and announced, "We just got a hit."

"Explain Spivey," said the Director.

"Just found this viral video that was uploaded on April 17. It has had over 24 million hits. It's a story from Austin, Texas. Some local news report investigating the problem one of the first winners, a Mexican national, had getting his money."

As they watched the video, it was apparent they had hit on something big. The Director looked up and announced, "Well boys. One of you is going to Austin, but let's call the local offices first," he said. "Good job, Spivey."

Andrews offered a weak congratulation to Spivey. He knew Spivey was only doing the IRS deal so that someday he could leave with those credentials on his resume. Someday he would begin his own tax accounting firm, probably fighting the IRS. While Andrews was the quintessential government man, dedicated to the IRS and his family (in that order); Spivey was just dedicated to Spivey.

***

"Chuckie Boy!" Screamed Zane French into the mic, "Get your big ass out here now . . . ! I'll make a deal with you. I'll keep playing tonight unless, unless, I see you stop dancing." Turning to his band, he instructs them with a "hit it" and the night began.

Charles acknowledged the singer and raised his hand in the air. Hours later he would be passed out on the floor.

Under the Puerto Rican sky, the night was going to prove to be festive. Will, Robert and Stu moved to the side and motioned for Ryan to join them. In many ways, Ryan was instrumental in helping launch the whole venture with the bogus news story. Will thought it a small form of payback to invite him to San Juan, although he did feel pretty awkward about flying Ryan's friend in as well. It never bothered him that Ryan was gay. He never gave it a second thought but seeing his partner made it come into reality. Will wondered if he were overly compensating in his acceptance of Ryan. No, he thought they were friends since grade school.

"Having fun?" asked Stu.

"Of course," said Ryan. "I needed to get away for a break. I really appreciate this, guys."

"Hey, don't thank us," said Robert. "We didn't even know about this trip until yesterday when we got to the airport."

"Thanks, Will," said Ryan.

"No problem, but I need to talk to you about something."

"Sure, anything for you, Will."

"Well, you know about our enterprise," Will spelled it out, "there's the three of us, Charles, one other, and then there is you."

"It's a pretty exclusive club, Ryan," said Stu in a harsh tone.

"I understand guys. You have no worries," said Ryan. "I'm solid."

"I understand," agreed Will as he pushed a large manila envelope towards him. "But, to show you our appreciation, here's a little something from us to you."

Opening the envelope Ryan discover a few bundles of money, he was astonished. "Guys, you don't have to do this. Are you trying to buy me off?" he asked. "I make very good money."

"That's not the point," said Robert. "Can you use it? Of course! Can you be a little, more wild than normal? Of course! Were you surprised? Yes. Then, enjoy."

Looking back over his shoulder, Will saw Charles out on the dance floor having the time of his life. With Charles and Cindy back together Will felt a little less guilt ridden over having been such a control freak.

Will was alone, yet full of peace.

***

"Andrews, I asked you in here because we have been speaking with foreign taxing entities and this thing is heating up," said the Director. "I am sending Spivey to Austin. I'll need you for something that will take advantage of your military background."

"I thought those days were over," joked Andrews.

"Not when your government needs you. I'll fill you in later."

***

Overlooking the vast ocean, a female worker on the top floor of the rig looked out at night. She was an attractive, young girl who had attracted the attention of a male co-worker. He had obviously been on *The Island* before, but the female was a newcomer to the rig and he was using his wisdom to woo her.

"See those lights over there?" he asked trying to impress her. "That's Cancun."

"Really? We are that far out?" she asked.

"Yeah, we are pretty far out here," he said. "Where are you from?"

"I was going to school in Austin but took this semester off to make some money," she answered. "Originally, I'm from Denver."

"Funny. My Mom's from there." Glad to score a point in this conversation, "Ever go back?"

"No, not since we moved to Austin six years ago," she said. "How many times have you done this shift?"

"I've done *The Island* four times," he said. "The money is pretty good."

"Yeah," she said sarcastically. "How much do you think they make here?"

"Mmm, best not to talk about that," he said. "That is the fastest way to get fired. It's in that agreement you signed."

"No. I don't want to lose the job," she said. Changing the subject, she asked, "Don't you ever worry being out here?"

"About what?" he asked more in an effort to keep the conversation going.

"What if a family member died or something? It's not like we can get calls out here or jump online when we're working," she said.

"Oh, I thought you were talking about the pirates out here," he said in hopes he could scare her into his arms. "See those lights out there? Probably drug cartel guys."

"The what?!" she demanded.

"There are no pirates out here," he said, trying to undo any damage he might have done. "Seriously, I don't think the cartels would be this far out either."

"This isn't helping," she said. "I'm going in."

"Whoa, whoa. . . . Don't go in," he pleaded. "I was just kidding."

She left and he was standing alone. "Dammit."

***

The phone rang and Will Sr. answered it in his bedroom. It was the private detective he hired some weeks ago. "Yes, Mr. Fairfield. This is a good time to talk."

"Mr. Hoke, I have the following information you requested. I have been very discreet and compiled the following information. I'll courier copies over to you later today."

"OK, let me get a pen and jot some of this down, in the mean time."

"Mr. Hoke, I have a William David Hoke born March 1989 with the following holdings one 2013 Mercedes SUV, a forty-one foot fishing vessel, a fifty-two foot Ocean Alexander speed boat, a 25% stake in an eight-seater Bell Helicopter to start." Fairfield took a break allowing Mr. Hoke a chance to get caught up before continuing. "A nightclub in Los Angeles—"

"Whoa, stop!" said Will Sr. "What part does he own in that?"

"One hundred percent," said Fairfield.

Clenching his fist and the phone, Will Sr. reluctantly asked him to continue.

"Bank accounts, I have a North Dallas Bank and Trust, and a Bank of America account, I have balances if you need," said Fairfield. "One odd thing I have not been able to confirm and will need more time to find out, there are multiple weekly deposits from a bank in the Caymans with amounts of $2,000 every other day. As you know, the Caymans are known for privacy. I may not be of much help here."

"This is fine," said an angry Will Sr. "I'll await the courier."

He then placed the phone down, and lowered his head fully aware that he had lost his son. He began to weep.

***

"Ladies and gentlemen, I hope you have had a great time here these last three days!" Will yelled out from the stage to the two hundred or so friends who had made the trip to San Juan. "We've partied, we've won some money, and some of you have lost some money, but all in all I hope you are having a great time. Now tonight is about my buddy, Robert—"

Interrupted by catcalls and cheers, Will acknowledged them and then continued, "To help me, do Robert's birthday right, I'll need a little help so let me now bring out his favorite actress Tracy Grace to help me. Tracy?! Tracy Grace!!"

An excited Robert was taken aback with unbridled enthusiasm. He had loved that actress since college. He jumped and pumped his fists in the air. Never in his wildest dreams had he thought this a possibility. Tracy Grace. Suddenly, he looked more attractive to every woman in the room and was now the envy of every male.

"Happy birthday, Robert," Tracy said and began to laugh. "I hope that tonight is as good as your desire is for me, which, by the way, since you'll never have me, your night better be great."

Turning to Will, she offered a high five making it obvious that the comment was staged. Robert sensed the joke on him and laughed and wondered if the night could get any better.

"Oh, and one more thing, Robert, your all time favorite band Bowling for Soup!!" Tracy enthusiastically announced.

The stage drew back revealing the band, but the band didn't play. Instead, the front man for the band, Jaret Reddick called out to Tracy. "Yo! Did you just diss my boy, Robbie here? On his birthday?"

Tracy stood there and soaked in the criticism and even appeared to bask in it.

"OK, song list change," Reddick informed the band. "The Bitch Song!"

The four-piece launched into their song and the place went up. Tracy stepped down off the stage and approached Robert. She was beautiful and she knew it.

"Happy Birthday, Robert Grissom."

"Thank you, umm, Tracy Grace," said a reserved Robert.

"Nice to see so many people care about you," she said. Robert wondered if she was being flirtatious or was he just on a high?

"Yeah, I've known him since junior high."

"He tells me that you are a billionaire, or he just trying to help you out with me?" she asked.

"Now why would you think I need to be helped out?" Robert smirked.

"Well for starters, I don't see a jealous girlfriend giving me the staredown."

"Maybe I was saving myself for you?"

"Oh, and you're pretty quick with a comeback. I am going to have to keep an eye on you."

"Tell me. Was that staged?" asked Robert, as the song was ending.

"About that, can you hold on for a sec?" Tracie asked as she went back onstage and joined the band.

"Tracy Grace everybody!" Reddick yelled. "Wrote that song about you!"

As the band launched into another tune, Tracy exited the stage once again to rejoin Robert.

"So, it was staged," said Robert.

"Oh, about that. I've known those guys for ten years. Met them at the Grammys and they are the soundtrack for one of my movies. They're crazy."

"Yeah, I met them in high school at a basketball game."

"So, what does a girl have to do to get a drink around here?"

"Silly me," Robert said. "Barkeep!"

Will was doing his best to mingle with everyone. He knew most of the group but there were a few he didn't know. A couple of women approached him with a look of awe.

"How did you get Tracy Grace to come to this party?" they asked.

"I own the Authority Bar in LA," said a cocky Will. "She comes there."

"Thank you so much for paying for all this," one of them said.

Will knows they are young, but so is the night, and Will is feeling confident. "Ladies, which one of you is single?"

***

As the Director sat before Spivey, he was more warm than usual. "I've got a job for you," he said. "I am sending you to Austin. I need to you speak with a reporter named Ryan Jensen. Reporters always protect their sources but sending someone from D.C. instead of a local office, might get him talking."

"OK, when do I leave?"

"You leave Thursday morning. Meet with the local agents, then, talk with Jensen that afternoon."

"Does he know I'm coming?"

"No. I think it best that we catch him off-guard."

"What about Andrews, sir? Is he coming too?"

"He has other orders."

***

Upon touching down in Dallas, Will stood up and addressed the passengers, "I want to thank all of you for coming out with us to celebrate Chuck and Robbie's birthdays. Now, whereas most of you didn't lose that much at the casinos, there were some of you that lost a lot. Sorry, but you will have to go back to work tomorrow and Friday to make up for your losses," he said. "Show your hand if you lost over 5 Gs."

One hand shot up and Will turned to Jimmy and quietly said, "Give him five. Discreetly." Will turned back to the others and said, "No photos. No Facebook or Instagram either, these last few days never happened or you won't be invited to the next trip for Stu's birthday. We might go to Monte Carlo!"

"Yeah, we didn't even have to use our passports!" yelled a passenger.

"Well, you had better watch it, Troy because I know where you live," laughed Will, he waved to him with a pistol point of his finger. "Seriously, get out of here. All of you. Bye, bye. Buh, bye. Ba, bye . . ."

As the group disembarked and began walking toward terminal, a heavy set black woman approached and screeched, "Oh my gosh, it *is* you!!" She said, "There are camera crews waiting for her!"

"How many?" asked Robert.

"Three or four cameras, but as many as ten people waiting," said the woman, who they now identified as an airport employee.

"When did Dallas get paparazzi?" asked Stu.

"Film festival is this week," said the woman.

"What is your name?" asked Robert.

"My name is Teresa."

"OK, Teresa. How much do you make a month at this job?" asked Will.

"First, what's it to ya? And—" She stopped at the sight of the envelope that Will produced, then continued. "I make about $2,200 a month."

"Here's three grand," said Will. "Let me see your drivers license and I'll double it—"

"OK, I can handle this," said Robert. "Tracy, are you OK with this?"

"Yes," she said.

"OK, then let everyone else go first and keep them away from the cameras," ordered Robert. Pulling Teresa aside, he said. "Your job is not to let one media person speak with any of them."

"Oh, I can handle that!" she said.

"Everybody!" Will commanded, "No media, please. Now go and we'll all talk soon."

Will turned to Tracy and her *handler* and explained, "I'll have your tickets changed and waiting for you at DFW. You'll be driven to the other airport." Pausing to text a message, he added. "We'll wait here until Jimmy comes around with the van and Charles collects their bags. Robert, you go with them and—"

"Yeah, about that Will," confided Robert as he lead Will away from the small group, "I wanna see where this is going.

Things went pretty good last night. I wanna go on to LA with her."

"Sure!" agreed Will.

"So, you're cool with it?" asked Robert.

"Dude, way to go!" praised Will. "If you don't go with her, I will!"

"I'll see you in a week or so," said Robert.

Meet an Agent

Ryan walked into his office and was taken aback at the sight of his news director and three unknown men in his office. His jovial thoughts of Puerto Rico and his tan had suddenly vanished and much like some of his former on-air guests, he was a deer in headlights.

"Ryan, these men are with the Internal Revenue Service and they are inquiring about a story you did, but for the life of me, I can't recall it," said the news director.

"I am Agent Roger Spivey in from D.C., these gentlemen are from our Austin offices," said Spivey.

"Nice to meet you," said Ryan, then gave an Oscar-worthy joke. "Or am I? I guess I now understand how people feel when *60 Minutes* shows up at their door." Pausing for a polite reply, but getting nothing, Ryan asked, "How can I help you or what have I done?"

"Mr. Jensen, we are interested in a news report you did about a Mexican national who was trying to collect some winnings from an online gaming site," Spivey said.

"Ryan, I told them that I don't recall us ever running a story like that," said the news director.

"We didn't," said Ryan, desperately trying to keep his cool. "We never ran it, there were too many inconsistencies in his story. You declined it."

"Well, do you mind then if we replay it for you? We have some questions relating to it," asked Spivey.

The news director looked at Ryan for his reaction and Ryan gave an OK to show it.

As the video played, the news director watched trying to recall the story. "I've never seen this report before," he declared. "Ryan?"

"I shot it downtown on two separate days and that was actually the night my office, this office, had been entered," said Ryan. "Remember, I even thought some things were missing."

"Seeing this again, Mr. Jensen do you remember anything the winner might have said, that's not in this video, about the website where he won his million?" asked one agent.

"No," said Ryan.

"Mr. Jensen, what we are really interested in is, just who is behind the website?" asked Spivey.

"I don't recall the individuals name. I can look through my notes," said a nervous Ryan. "It was all very clandestine, very secretive. I recall we corresponded by texts or emails, never on the phone. He said he would be in the States in a few days and we shot him then. He demanded that the cameras never show his face and that the room be dark. We shot it in only a few minutes and then he was gone. Never heard from him again."

"Mr. Jensen, I can't help but notice that you wore the same outfit in both shots," said Spivey. "Was this report all done in one day? One would assume that wardrobe would be pretty important to a reporter—"

"I only shot my scenes after I interviewed the website rep."

"Yes, that is not unusual," affirmed the news director.

"But, what is unusual is we have been tracking this online site to check any status of U.S. involvement and Mr. Jensen here is the only person we have found anywhere that has had direct contact with them," said Spivey.

"Look, at the time we didn't know what this was," explained Ryan. "If I had known how big this was going to get, I would have dug deeper and could have made it a national story. *Every* reporter looks for that national story. If you are trying to embarrass me in front of my boss here, then mission accomplished."

"Why then did you travel to the Cayman Islands in September for the worldwide press conference?" asked Spivey. "According to your boss here, you asked to fly to the Caymans to cover it."

"Well, I did feel I had a valid reason since I had the story you just had us watch," reasoned Ryan. "I hoped to use that to get an exclusive interview, you know, get that national story, but I wasn't granted one."

"Kind of odd, I guess, that a station that is only in the Top 40 of the U.S. media market would pay so much attention to this unless there was more to it," said Spivey, who looked around the room only to realize that he was the only non-Austinite there and quickly added, "No disrespect to your fine city."

With that, the news director stood up and asked, "Mr. Spivey, is there anything more we can do for you?" He seemed perturbed that his time was being taken up by this IRS *gang*. And Ryan found it odd that his boss was defending him.

"No, I guess we are finished . . . for now. Gentlemen, we appreciate your time," said Spivey. "We'll be in touch."

"Thank you for understanding," said the news director.

Stopping at the door, Spivey asked one last question, "By the way, Mr. Jensen, where did you go for your vacation?"

Stunned at the request, and knowing they could access his phone record and credit cards records and prove his attendance in Puerto Rico, Ryan hesitated. He knew this was a gotcha question. "I stayed local, right here in Texas," he replied. Was it to his undoing? Only time would tell.

As the agents left, the news director stared at Ryan, trying to *read* him. Ryan looked away.

"I sure hope you haven't compromised yourself."

***

On the pad in Corpus, the guys buckled up in the helicopter. The foursome was beginning to be at ease with leaving *The Island*. Stu was the first to inquire about business. "How many winners now?"

"We have 28,200-something. At this pace, we'll hit the magic number of 30,000 well before our one year anniversary," said Will.

"How'd we do while we were away?"

Checking his phone for reports, Will replied, "Since we left almost six days ago, we have had 686 winners. So that made us over $120 mil net while we were away."

"Divided by four, right?" asked Charles.

"Yes," said Will. "And that makes up for the $800 Gs I spent on you and Robert this week."

"Oh c'mon, Will," complained Charles. "Why don't you tell us what you spent on us. How classy."

"Hey, at least Robert is still enjoying his," said Stu. "Seriously Will, I can wait 'til my birthday comes around. April 6th by the way."

"Do you think we're getting sloppy?" asked Charles.

"Like how?" asked Stu.

"You know good and well, Stu," snapped Charles. "We've had two major blowouts in a month and they were border lining on being pretty public. I thought we were still trying to fly under the radar."

"So, what are you getting at?" asked Will.

"You bought a club at the drop of the hat. Yeah, we know," Charles stated. "It made the papers and people will talk. Now you score Tracy Grace for Robert?!"

"Hey, I just introduced them. If they hit it off, that was strictly their own deal."

"Well when we started this, it was to make some money but the key thing was to be discreet," said Charles. "Discreet. We're not being discreet."

"I didn't plan it that way and I understand, it's just too easy with what we have access to," said Will.

"Well, I'd rather be rich that famous," said Charles. "I actually know some famous poor people."

"We were already rich to begin with," said Stu.

***

Agent Wilson walked into the Director's office without waiting for an invite. The Director looked up at her for an explanation.

"We have discovered the exact location of the lottery's operational headquarters," she announced.

***

Stepping off the helicopter, Will was approached by a female worker. She had a look of concern on her face and pulled Will aside.

"Problem?" Will asked.

"Possibly," she said. "A few days ago we had an odd occurrence. We had someone put $600,000 in one jackpot."

"A one-time amount or over several plays?"

"A one-time amount," she confirmed. "We thought there was a technical problem but we verified it. The funds actually cleared—"

"And?" snapped Will, wanting her to get to the point.

"Well, they won."

"Well, that was either pretty stupid or ballsy," said Will. "Now, that is a gambler. I guess it paid off."

"There's more," she cautiously came to the real issue. "This particular person was in Yemen."

"Oh, but we've had winners from there before."

"Yes, but now we have had eight more wins all played using a similar strategy," she said.

"What!?"

"Actually nine attempts since Sunday with eight being winners. We had seen an increase in players since the Christmas gift cards, but those had an expiration date and that ends at midnight tonight. We were so busy we didn't catch it all at first. When we ran all the numbers this afternoon, we couldn't reach you."

"Are they all from Yemen?"

"No, there are three from Yemen, four from Saudi Arabia and two from the U.S. All using the same strategy. Some times they do $200,000 between three or four players. It's a very precise system they have.

"A U.S./Middle East connection . . . this is trouble," admitted Will.

***

Agent Spivey walked down the hallway talking on his phone. On the other end was Agent Andrews. Spivey had called to smooth things over.

"John, I'm back in D.C. from Austin," said Spivey.

"How'd that go?" asked Andrews.

"Well, either that reporter just got lucky and did an interview when this thing was in its infant stage and knows nothing or he's a good actor."

"What's your guess?" asked Andrews. In the background, several loud bangs—in rapid succession—could be heard.

"I don't really know," said Spivey, hesitating to try and determine what those bangs might have been. "Listen, John. I feel kinda bad about getting this Austin trip when you've been heading this up. I never meant to usurp this gig."

"Trust me. We're good."

"Are you at the firing range?"

"I guess you could say that," said Andrews, as he acknowledged to Navy SEALs that he was ready.

"Sir, you are up," said one of the SEALs.

"Look, I need to go but thanks for the call—"

***

Alone in his office, Will Sr. picked up the phone and made a call.

"National Bank of the Caymans."

"Yes, this is William Hoke and I was calling for a balance on my accounts."

"Yes, Mr. Hoke. May I have your account number?"

"That's why I am calling. I'm not at my computer and need to check the balance because I might be making a big purchase.

If we could be quick and discreet, I would appreciate it," said Will Sr.

"May I have the ID number from your passport, Mr. Hoke?"

Fumbling through the various papers the private investigator had supplied, he came upon his son's passport information. He read the numbers out for verification.

"Issued where?"

"Houston, on July 6, 2009."

"OK," the banker continued. "Date of birth, mother's maiden name and make of your first car."

Will Sr. knew all the right answers.

"What can I do for you?"

"I need a balance tally."

"Do you want an approximate amount or the exact amount?"

"Approximate would be fine."

"Fine," said the banker. "Sir, we have never met and I look forward to meeting you someday. Can you hold for a few minutes?"

"Certainly," Not as private as one would think he thought. Then again, the young woman seemed very eager to please. Was his son, his namesake, a gigolo or highly prized catch down there?

It was approximately 5 minutes before she came back on the line and apologized for the wait. "In all accounts, that would be in the range of $638 U.S. dollars, sir."

"638?" repeated Will Sr. slightly confused. "Is that all?"

"Well, as I see in the notes, this does not reflect the other $371 million coming from the Swiss accounts this week. They have yet to post it," she corrected.

Writing the numbers down and doing a quick add, he was amazed. How? Where? He added up the numbers and it came to 1,009 . . . $1,009 billion U.S.!

"Mr. Hoke?" He heard her calling out to him. "Mr. Hoke? Are you there?"

"Yes. Yes," he said fighting back his anxiety. "I'll have to call back." He hurriedly turned and tried to slow his breathing, then he reached for the trash can and vomited.

***

A stoic Will sat the guys down in the main office. He relayed to them what he had just learned about players possibly gaming the system. They could tell that his no holds barred fearless approach in San Juan had been replaced by panic. Whatever this was, it had Will scared.

"Basically, what this means is, that someone has not only figured out how to hedge their bets with a 3 to 1 ratio of winning, it means fewer players will be playing," Will said. "This will affect our bottom line and could—"

"So, we drop from making $180,000 a jackpot to a little over $100,000 per, we'll still be doing fine," Stu interrupted.

"No the money is still the same," said Charles.

"You don't get it!" said Will. "I see four problems. First, someone has figured out a way to win, a way that only a handful of people can afford . . . who are they? Second, many of these winners are coming from the Middle East . . . terrorist countries. And third, there are U.S. players using the same strategy which means either they are linked or something is going on out there that we are not in control of. Lastly, if the U.S. is monitoring the players in those Middle Eastern countries, then the focus will turn to us soon enough."

"I'm not so certain," said Charles. "Have you ever bought gas where the owner is from the Middle East? Or gone to a club back home owned by some possible Muslims? Did you worry then that you were implicated?"

"I say we just take a wait and see attitude," said Stu.

"Well, here is the part you don't know," Will said. "They wanted the money sent to banks in Dubai and the Emirates, not Cayman or Swiss banks. That worries me."

"Crap," said Charles. "That isn't good."

***

"We've been watching our friends over the weekend," said the Director. "I have Andrews in a special training session preparing to end all of this, yet I have no news from you."

Spivey thought for a moment then said, "We are being patient."

"It troubles me to learn that there are 112 recent winners coming from what could only be described as terrorist states. That is over $100 million dollars to support their various activities all provided by what just might turn out to be U.S. citizens. That bothers me."

"Of course," was all Spivey could offer.

"I can't afford to be patient, and, neither can you."

Stock Pile

In an effort to be proactive, Will and the guys created an emergency plan in case of any intrusion, attack, or hurricane. Over the Christmas break, Will had brought in a group of construction workers to expand the living quarters, improve the entertainment room and create escape routes to the boats and the helipad.

The lottery workers did not question the improvements to the living quarters or the entertainment room but they did have questions about the escape routes. They asked Will if there was some threat that they were not aware of. Will said no, and told them it was in case of fire or hurricane. Explaining that all working rigs now have escape plans.

Standing down by the boat, Charles acted as tour guide. He explained where the chute came out in reference to the water and the boats. It was then that the boat, which had visited the rig before, approached. By the time they were aware of its presence, it was too late to do anything but just stand there. Not wanting to look afraid, Charles demanded that everyone stay where they were.

"Still here, *amigo*?" the man said. He was a weathered man in his 30s, and there was an air of confidence about him that even out here in the middle of nowhere, you sensed he was in charge.

"Yeah, we are still here with the university," said Stu. "Studying the fish."

"It must get lonely out here."

"Not really," said Stu. "We are always on the phone back to the states."

"Maybe you should take a break and allow us to come onboard and party," he said, laughing aloud. "Maybe we bring some women to even things out."

"That's why they always have the cameras on us," replied Stu, in an effort to discourage any thought of boarding the rig. "The *Federales* are always watching."

With that the Mexican's smile departed. "So why you wear all the same clothes?" he asked pointing to the workers.

"Regulations," said Stu. "For the laboratory."

"*Laboratorio*," said one of the workers.

"*Si, si, claro,"* said the Mexican, as he continued to look around the massive rig, suspiciously eyeing the fixtures. This made everyone a little nervous, including Stu. To lighten the mood, he offered.

"There is a lot of ocean out there, you be careful, OK?"

"OK, my friends," the Mexican said as he ordered the driver to pull away.

No one said anything until he well away from the rig.

"Well, that was weird, just to drop in like that," said one worker.

"No, that was scary!" said another.

"Let's go, everyone," said Charles. "Let's go back up top. I think our escape tour has ended"

"Again? What's a boat that small doing way out here?" Stu asked directing his question toward Charles.

***

Seated across from his boss, Ryan was at ease, but he knew that this guy didn't like him. Maybe it was the way he had pushed for stories as a cub reporter or maybe he didn't like his lifestyle but he was in Austin, Texas, the most liberal city in the South. Sure, he defended him with the IRS agents but what did he want?

"Ryan, I want you to tell me everything you know about this Mundo Lottery site," said the news director.

"Sir, I did a story on them. We couldn't validate everything but still I did offer it to you, but you said *no*," Ryan said sticking to his story. "My office was ransacked, remember? And now that used footage has gone viral and no one seemed to care. And now, the IRS shows up acting as if I'm the bad guy?"

"Oh, shut up. I was there for you," he said. "We don't leave our reporters in the lurch."

"Yes, and thank you for that sir," said Ryan. He hesitated then admitted, "There were some personal things taken that night. Things maybe not everyone knows about me—"

"Forget that. I think you know more. Now, tell me. What did we pay for when we sent you down to the Caymans in September?"

***

"Charles, my man! How's it out there on *The Island*?" asked Robert, who was reclining in the sun by the pool.

"I wouldn't know you since you've become a Hollywood star banging lothario," said Charles.

"Hey, watch it," Robert cautioned. "Are you still making us rich?"

"No, I'm out here blowing all our money," said a laughing Charles.

"Well, hold off on blowing all of it," laughed Robert.

"No prob."

"Seriously though, I'm going to stay in LA for another week or so—" Hearing the sound of rapid gunfire, Charles asked, "What is going on there? Is that Will?"

"No, that's Stu *and* Will," said Charles. "We had visitors today. Nothing big."

"Really? Do you need me to hire security people?"

"No, we're OK," said Charles. "Hey, and about staying out there in LA, that's no problem, I'm going to spend more time in Dallas with Cindy now, too."

"Good for you," said Robert. "And good for her. I always liked her."

"Tell me though, can you send me some nude pics of Tracy? I'm all spent searching online."

"Bye, Charles." And Robert hung up.

Charles roared in his own laughter.

***

"So, they are in the Gulf of Mexico, on an abandoned oil rig, just over 200 miles from the U.S. coast," said the Director. "Are they fronting Al-Qaeda? ISIS? Someone else? We've got *winners* in the Middle East and every known *terrorist nation*. Maybe, this lottery was just a clever front."

"There has been gunfire from the rig. That has been confirmed," said an agent seated at the table.

"Spivey, what do you know of this?" asked the Director.

"There is drug activity in the region but that rig belongs to a Thomas Bay, who is in his '70s and I seriously doubt—"

"Actually, that was sold to a group or someone in Houston called Hogris Baysew in October," said the subordinate.

"So, what are you saying?" asked the Director.

"That is an anagram for Boyish Wagers," said the subordinate. "Clever, I guess."

"No, this group intentionally parks themselves in our backyard and sets up shop, not in Cuba. Not in Mexico or South America but on an oil rig just miles from our coastline," stated the Director. "Not on my time. Not on my watch. Get me the Pentagon."

***

On a well guarded plantation in Mexico, a *soldier* walked among the workers. Many were attending to business, but a man (the man from the boat) spotted a worker on his phone. He went and confronted the worker about his laziness and lack of productivity. He did this in effort to gain favor with the *jefe.*

"What are you doing?" he demanded in Spanish.

The young man answered in a pleading voice that he was simply waiting to view the winners of the lottery. "*Si, en momentos tienen un ganador,*" said the worker explaining that there would soon be a winner.

Then, in an effort to mock and ridicule the worker, the man from the boat yelled for all to take notice. Then, as he took possession of the phone, he saw the screen and on it he saw the jackpot. He saw the money. "How much to win?" he asked.

"These guys pay out millions of dollars each day."

Mesmerized, he asked even more questions.

"They have a live feed you can watch," the worker said taking back the phone. When he handed it back, the live feed filled the screen.

Immediately the man from the boat noticed the clothes. The clothes he saw only yesterday. "I know where this is!" he exclaimed. "I know who these people are!"

***

"Close the door behind you, Spivey," said the Director. Motioning the young agent to sit down. The Director had a more than usual serious look, and got straight to the point. "After 9/11 our government began to operate on a proactive basis. If we see a threat, we would rather confront it than have to react to a first strike. In this case, we have determined that this gaming site has aided in the funding of terrorist cells. We also believe that at least one U.S. citizen is involved. And it is all being done right under our noses in the Gulf of Mexico.

"At pre-dawn, U.S. forces will be taking into custody any U.S. nationals found aboard the oil rig we have determined to be the headquarters of Mundo Lottery."

"So, we have located the exact spot of this operation?" asked Spivey.

"It's an oil rig based less than 200 damned miles from the U.S. coastline."

"And if it's not occupied with U.S. citizens might there be an international incident?"

"All the more reason we need to know who this is," said the Director. "The people at the Pentagon don't want to be explaining another attack on the U.S. One that, in this case, could have been prevented."

"Why are you telling me this and not John?"

"Who do you think will be accompanying the SEALs in tomorrow's raid?"

***

"So, I hear you have some big news for me," said Jorge (El Jefe) Parades.

"Yes sir," said the man from the boat. "For the past few months when I patrol the Gulf making checks and drop offs, I spotted an oil rig with people on it. I had approached them before asking who they were. They told me they were college students studying fish with the U.S. government. This was a lie. Yesterday, I saw one of the workers on that lottery site on the computer. The one that pays out millions. I recognized the people in the video. They are the ones who are on the rig!"

"So, what are you saying?"

"There has to be many millions on that rig. One of the workers said it could even be billions. And we, I mean you, could take it."

"Take what? I doubt there would be money out on that rig."

"Sir, I have witnessed helicopters landing there and they have a top of the line speedboat. These are no ordinary college kids. They have to have computers and surely they must have access to all that money some way."

"How long have you known this?" asked El Jefe. "You seem pretty smart and more useful than what I have been using you for."

"I had my suspicions for some time, but yesterday, it all became very clear," said the boater. "I immediately requested to speak with you."

"I am a man that rewards loyalty. What is your name?"

"Carlos."

"Well, Carlos. You can now prove yourself even more worthy by verifying what you have said. I will give you up to twelve men, a proper boat and twenty-four hours to report back to me. You might have just made not only us all richer, but yourself a very rich man."

"Thank you, sir," said Carlos.

"I suggest you get started," said El Jefe.

***

"Any news?" asked Stu.

"No, I did call Bob Patterson for help," said Will. "I told him I'd be in town next week."

"How much are you going to tell him?" asked Stu.

"I think we're going to have to claim something to explain for upcoming taxes," said Will. "April 15th is coming up."

"Yeah, I've been debating that one, too," said Charles.

Will caught a glimpse of something that angered him. He reached out on the desk and grabbed the thumb drive and held it up. "Who left the master drive out?!" he demanded.

"It was there when I came in here," said Charles.

"Yeah, I thought you were working on something," agreed Stu.

Will stormed out of the office and began to confront the one he suspected of leaving it out. Everyone could hear him yelling but chose to remain out of it. Will returned to the office. Before anyone could address the issue, he said,. "She left the master drive out with information of over $30 billion dollars on it!! Just left it out to be lost and the safe is two feet away—"

"Will, she left it *out* in the office," said Charles in an attempt to calm Will's mood.

"Just remember, it also has almost 4 billion which is ours," said Will as he exited the room.

"Yeah, now that you point that out," said Charles.

Will sat stewing in anger while Charles and Stu exchanged glances.

"I think he's losing it," whispered Stu.

***

Will Sr. sat alone in his home contemplating what his life had become. He thought of his son, his namesake and recalled the times he missed while the kids were growing up. How he had become a slave to his work and how he had missed out on so many things. Maybe it was the fact that Jimmy was marrying and the family would grow but no, he knew that his estrangement with Will had fostered a resentment that now had his eldest son involved in something sinister. Had he driven his son to into the drug trade? How else did Will get all that money?

He picked up the phone to call Will. In his anxiety, he took a deep breath for discernment. Part of him wanted to scream and shout accusations and the other wanted him to beg his son's forgiveness.

He dialed Will's number. It went straight to voice mail. Hearing his little boy's voice, he choked up a little, but regained his composure in time to leave a message.

"Son, this is your Dad. I know it's late and we haven't spoken in weeks but I wanted to give you a call to say I was thinking of you. I also wanted to say how proud that I am of you and tell you something that I haven't said to you since, I guess we brought you home from the hospital, but son, I love you. Your mom and I both love you and I know she tells you, but it's time that I did too. No, I'm not dying, it's just something I wanted to say. Goodbye, son."

He hung up and blew a big sigh of relief.

***

Will approached the worker and she had a frightened look in her eye. Seeing this, Will held out his hand showing that he was coming in peace.

"Hey, look, I'm sorry about the blow up today. I was wrong about that."

"No, it's OK," she said.

Laughing, he said, "No, it's not. I'm just dealing with a lot of things right now."

"I had a boyfriend that used to yell a lot—"

"Still, no excuse," Will offered. "Are we OK?"

"Yeah, we are OK," she confirmed. "Listen, there is something that I wanted to tell you anyway."

"Yeah?"

"Earlier this week, you wanted to know when we hit a particular number . . ."

"And . . ."

"We should hit that number sometime during the night."

"Excellent," said Will. "Listen, whatever time it is, I want you or whoever to wake me, no all of us, wake us all."

"Will do," she said. "Any time?"

"Any."

Let's All Meet

Will approached the guys and announced that he had great news.

"What's up?" asked Charles.

"Tonight, we will hit the magic number!"

"The magic number?" asked Charles.

"Yep," said Will. "Tonight we officially become billionaires! Each of us!"

"Awesome," said Stu, who stood to offer high fives.

"Get this," added Will, "I told the workers to pipe 'Bitter Sweet Symphony' throughout the rig when we hit that mark. Bittersweet because we're billionaires but can't tell anybody."

"Bittersweet, because we're way the hell out here in the ocean," said Charles.

"Well Chuckie, those days will be over shortly. I promise."

***

In the dark of night, a small band of soldiers made their way from the ship into a small inflatable boat. They number eight, made up of seven Navy SEALS and one IRS agent with a military background—one IRS Agent John Andrews.

The motor started and they pulled away from the ship and headed out into the darkness.

***

One worker sat watching the monitors and checking the progress, the total reached 29,998 total winners.

"Just two more before I'm supposed to wake up the guys," the worker said. "A milestone they want to witness."

***

A speedboat raced into the darkness that was the Gulf of Mexico. At the helm was Carlos who, courtesy of El Jefe, found himself in charge of a dozen other men.

The boat was of enough size that Carlos had to yell as he explained the layout of the massive rig. The plan was to come within fifty feet of the rig, coast in, then quietly board while those on the rig slept.

***

Now within sight of the rig, the SEALS killed the motor and came to a stop. Using hand gestures to communicate, and equipped infrared vision, they slipped into the water. Andrews' heart was racing as he followed his new comrades into the dark uncertainty. They dropped several feet below the water and employed their personal propulsion devices for the next quarter mile.

***

"Wake up, Will," she said, gently pushing on his shoulder. "Wake up. You are one jackpot away."

Despite having downed a couple of beers before going to sleep, Will surged from his slumber and knocked on the other rooms. "Get up!" he commanded. "This is the moment."

As she followed him down the hall, Will was still trying to clear the cobwebs from his head, but he was ecstatic. Everyone who had ever questioned his resolve, intelligence or ambition, would have to take it all back. It was his now point, set, match.

As the clock ticked to 5:21 a.m., the *pot* continued to fill, just as it had done over 29,999 times before. Somewhere in the world of 7 billion people, a new millionaire would soon be created and four young men would join the Billionaires Club.

Never mind that the sun had yet to rise, each popped a beer and toasted what seemed to be happening in slow motion.

Finally, the millionth ticket was bought and the goal was reached!

Although Will had given this number, the goal had been reached a month before but the greed of *owning more* had infected Will. It was his secret. It was a BILLION plus, baby!!

"Come out on the platform," Will said as he grabbed a couple of AR15 rifles and handed them to Charles and Stu. He grabbed a big paper sack and commanded, "Follow me."

As they made their way onto the platform, one worker turned to the rest and said, "I don't get the significance of that number." Seeing that no one else did either, they resumed their boring duties.

"Charles, I guess you can buy that football team you've always wanted," said Stu.

"Not the one I want," Charles said.

"Hey, we need to call Robert," said Stu.

"He's probably too smitten to care," said Will. "Maybe we should have split his money last week then we'd have been off this rig sooner."

"Not funny," said Stu.

Standing on the rig's top platform firing, they let out a celebratory screams. Will fumbled through the paper bag pulling out the fireworks as he walked over to the hallway and yelled, "Cue the music and make sure it's out here!" he yelled.

The aptly titled "Bitter Sweet Symphony" by The Verve began playing on speakers throughout the rig. Since Will had planned for most everyone to be awake, the volume was set on high.

Bullets ripped into the night's darkness with little concern. Aiming at the stars, Will emptied his magazine as shell casing dropped at his feet. Stu aimed into the water and let go a circular pattern in the ocean below.

***

Twenty feet below, in the water, the Navy SEALs surfaced to the commotion above them. The silence was broken. The lead SEAL called through his mic, "We've been compromised! Gunfire detected! Do we abort? Sir! Do we abort?"

***

Robert sat staring at his laptop. Will had told him about the landmark and he couldn't sleep. Tonight was the night.

Having just come home from a night out with Tracy, he was wide-awake anyway. He lowered the volume so he could just hear "Bitter Sweet Symphony" playing and nodded as he minimized the screen to check his email and surf the web.

He looked back at his sleeping beauty and grinned. He was so happy not to be on that rig. He was right where ever single male wanted to be. What a lucky guy.

***

The water around the rig began to light up due to the Roman candle fireworks that Will had fired into the water, the threesome continued to light up the sky. Shooting into the darkness, Charles put his rifle down and grabbed the fireworks from Will and launched a Roman candle in the air. As it lit up the Gulf sky, the cartel boat become exposed.

"We've got company!" panicked Stu, pointing to the boat that was now speeding toward the rig. Hearing the triumphant hullabaloo, the cartel had changed plans and decided to launch a hasty assault, since it was obvious the people on the rig were not asleep. In an effort to deter the oncoming boat, Will fired in their direction unknowingly coming within striking distance of the cartel. Stu fired into the sea.

Confusion abounded.

The lead SEAL called back to the ship again, "Sir! Again, we are being fired upon!!" No one responded.

Seeing the crew from the boat boarding the rig, the threesome retreated back inside in a panic. They had taken some vain, ineffective shots, but these trust fund kids weren't killers.

"Who are they?!" yelled Charles.

"Lock the doors below!" yelled Stu.

"There are no locks on the stairway doors!!" yelled Will. "Have everyone get out! Now!"

The SEALs boarded the rig from the East and began to secure the first floor.

Meanwhile, the cartel charged up the stairwell in a brute sprint from the West.

One lone SEAL raced from the opposite side to establish a lookout position.

Charles raced into the "web room" and ordered, "Get out! Everyone out of here!"

At first the workers just sat there, then Charles yelled, "Take the chute to the boat! This is no joke. Take the chute just like we showed you!"

"What's going on?" asked one of the female workers.

"There are people on the rig and they have guns!" With that proclamation, chaos ensued.

From one side of the rig, the cartel began beating down doors, while, unbeknownst to anyone, four SEALs made their way to the third floor.

Will, Charles and Stu huddled in fear debating whether to join the workers who were fleeing to safety or fight back.

As workers emerged from the chute with hopes of departing on the boat, they were met by Andrews and another SEAL, who drew down on them.

Three members of the cartel remained on the deck, where the music and turmoil made it impossible for them to hear if anyone was approaching, suddenly catching a glimpse of men with guns, the cartel members fired on the SEALs. The SEALs returned fire killing two of them.

***

Robert clicked back to the Mundo Lottery website and found it odd that no one was on the screen. He wondered why that was.

***

Awakened by all the commotion, Hector opened the door and peered out from his room. His wife took a quick peek to see what all the fuss was about then ran back to her bed.

Hector admonish the trespassers in vivid Spanish. Realizing who the attackers were his bravado disappeared. Now he feared for his life. As he made eye contact with the gunman, his panic became even more evident. He had no gun. He had no chance. The gunman raised his weapon, and fired—the gun misfired.

***

Will yelled to Charles to go down to the dock with the others then turned to Stu, "I have to go get the drive!" Will raced down the hall and felt the wiz of several bullets as they passed near his head. He turned and fired uncertain where the shots had actually come from.

***

Transfixed by what he was seeing and wondered if this wasn't some prank or joke, staged just for him, Robert was caught between fear and amusement. Just as he reached for his phone and began to dial the private line to the rig, an errant bullet tore through one of the computer screens. That was followed by a male diving into the empty room. It was forbidden to show one's face on the webcast but that diving male was Will, for all the world to see. Robert watched as Will moved around to the desk where the night manager sat, retrieved the thumb drive and then he was gone from the screen. By now Robert was pretty sure he was not being pranked.

***

Now the remaining cartel members were amassed on one side, the SEALs poised on the other, with Will and Stu, in the office, stuck in the middle. Will took the master thumb drive and placed it into a plastic Ziploc bag.

"What are you doing?" demanded Stu.

"Getting all the money," snapped Will. "I'm not letting whoever this is shooting at us, get it and since I may have to go in the water, I don't want it to get ruined."

Charles heard the shots coming from below, but could not stop his momentum down the chute and he came crashing onto the deck, rifle in hand. Andrews and the SEAL had made a positive identification that these unarmed workers were Americans making them hesitant to fire on anyone else coming down the shoot. So by the time they realized Charles had a gun, it was too late. Charles let loose dropping the SEAL and wounding Andrews. Andrews fired back hitting Charles as both dropped to the ground. The few remaining workers who were unwounded, scrambled to find cover.

Hearing gunfire from the other side of the rig, a cartel member lifted a Stinger missile upon his shoulder and fired. The missile struck a steel support leg causing the rig to shift.

Peaking around the corner, Stu saw the cartel and turned to inform Will, "It's that weird guy from the boat." Will moved hoping for a glimpse. The cartel unloaded more rounds. Will and Stu returned fire down the hall and pulled back for cover.

"Who are you?" yelled Will. "What do you want?"

Will turned to Stu for support only to find him curled up in a fetal position.

Another burst of gunfire from the cartel went unanswered by Will. Then from the opposite direction another set of gunfire erupted.

"Identify yourself!" demanded the SEAL leader. The cartel fired back at the SEAL, who reported back to the ship, "Sir, this unit is being protected by apparent Mexican nationals, possibly a cartel."

"Then, fire at will," ordered the ship's captain. "But take as many alive as you can."

***

Back in LA, Robert watched in horror as he saw the camera shake and the picture tilt.

***

Impatient with the standoff, the cartel members prepared to charge the hall. As they begin their assault down the hall, the Navy SEALs opened fire, killing six more cartel members. Only Carlos remained. Realizing that he had lost at least eight of his twelve men, he raced back toward his boat.

Carlos had botched his first big opportunity and El Jefe would not be happy. Everyone had to go. Grabbing the RPG, he ordered his remaining two men to level the rig.

Sensing an opening, Will turned to Stu yelling, "Let's go!" And he raced toward the chute. Turning to ensure that Stu was behind one, he saw no one. Stu had remained in the room.

With the Navy SEALs firing upon him and he had no choice, he went headfirst down the chute.

Backing away from the rig, Carlos and the two remaining cartel fighters took aim on the rig and fired. They hit the steel supports. The rig rocked. Carlos aimed for the top floor and fired, producing multiple explosions. As the rig lurched forward, the chute carrying Will changed direction.

The SEAL, who had been positioned in the lookout spot, fired a grenade that took out Carlos and his henchmen in a fiery explosion.

Twenty years of neglect sitting in the Gulf, a few well placed Stinger missiles, and the rig snapped. It only took a few seconds for the once massive rig to crash into the water taking everyone still onboard with it.

***

Robert, unable to reach anyone on the phone, began running his fingers through his hair in fear and disbelief. Then, the webcam went dead.

***

From a half a mile away, the sailors aboard the Navy ship watched the rig light up the Gulf as it exploded. Repeated calls and orders went unanswered.

***

Robert sat with tears in his eyes over what he had just witnessed. What had he just witnessed?

***

With morning now breaking into the darkness, smoke and debris marked the spot where just a few hours ago stood a massive oil rig. There was silence, and no one to hear it. Nary a life in sight.

There were no heroes, no villains. No billions, no laughter, just the eerie echo of death and destruction.

There was however a plastic Ziploc bag containing two USB thumb drives. Thumb drives that contained access to billions of dollars. Billions that had come from an idea that a young man and his friends had brought to life. A young man who had to prove his worth to himself, to his father, and to a lost love who never knew how much he still cared. An idea that had caused the loss of at least thirty lives, thirty families all affected by money and greed.

As the Ziploc bag floated in the early morning at the spot where an oil rig, turned Mundo Lottery headquarters, once stood, a single hand reached up out of the water and snagged it.

Made in the USA
Charleston, SC
13 November 2014